DISCARD

Science Behind Sports

Basketball

Science on the Court

By Emily Mahoney

Portions of this book originally appeared in *Basketball* by Diane Yancey.

Published in 2018 by
Lucent Press, an Imprint of Greenhaven Publishing, LLC
353 3rd Avenue
Suite 255
New York, NY 10010

Designer: Seth Hughes
Editor: Katie Kawa

Cataloging-in-Publication Data

Names: Mahoney, Emily.
Title: Basketball: Science on the Court / Emily Mahoney.
Description: New York : Lucent Press, 2018. | Series: Science behind sports | Includes index.
Identifiers: ISBN 9781534561083 (library bound) | ISBN 9781534561090 (ebook)
Subjects: LCSH: Basketball–Juvenile literature.
Classification: LCC GV885.1 M22 2018 | DDC 796.323–dc23

Printed in the United States of America

CPSIA compliance information: Batch #BS17KL: For further information contact Greenhaven Publishing LLC, New York, New York at 1-844-317-7404.

Please visit our website, www.greenhavenpublishing.com. For a free color catalog of all our high-quality books, call toll free 1-844-317-7404 or fax 1-844-317-7405.

Contents

Foreword 4

Chapter 1: 6
From Humble Beginnings to Worldwide Fame

Chapter 2: 18
Training for Results

Chapter 3: 32
Injuries: Sidelining Star Athletes

Chapter 4: 47
Gear for the Game

Chapter 5: 58
Physics and Basketball

Chapter 6: 74
The Biomechanics of Basketball

Chapter 7: 83
The Future of the Game

Notes 95
Glossary 100
For More Information 101
Index 103
Picture Credits 111
About the Author 112

Foreword

When people watch a sporting event, they often say things such as, "That was unbelievable!" or "How could that happen?" The achievements of superstar athletes often seem humanly impossible—as if they defy the laws of nature—and all sports fans can seemingly do is admire them in awe.

However, when a person learns the science behind sports, the unbelievable becomes understandable. It no longer seems as if athletes at the top of their game are defying the laws of nature to achieve greatness; it seems as if they are using the laws of nature to their fullest potential. This kind of knowledge might be thought by some to take away from a pure appreciation of sports, but that is far from the truth. Understanding the science that makes athletic achievements possible allows fans to gain an even deeper appreciation for athletic performances and how athletes use science to their advantage.

This series introduces readers to the scientific principles behind some of the world's most popular sports. As they learn about physics concepts such as acceleration, gravity, and kinetic versus potential energy, they discover how these concepts can be applied to pitches in baseball, flips in gymnastics, dunks in basketball, and other movements in a variety of sports. In addition to the physics behind amazing plays, readers discover the science behind basic training and conditioning for different sports, the biology involved in understanding common sports injuries and their treatments, and the technological advances paving the way for the future of athletics.

The scientific concepts presented in this series are explained using accessible language and engaging examples. Complicated principles are simplified through the use of detailed diagrams, charts, graphs, and a helpful glossary. Quotations from scientists, athletes, and coaches give readers a firsthand perspective, and further research is encouraged through a detailed bibliography and a list of additional resources.

Athletes, sports fans, and budding scientists will get something important out of this series: information about how to exercise and fuel the body to excel in competition, a deeper appreciation for the history of their favorite sport, and a stronger understanding of how science works in the world around us.

The worlds of science and sports are not as far apart as they may seem. In fact, sports could not exist without science. In understanding the relationship between these two worlds, readers will become more knowledgeable sports fans and better athletes.

Chapter 1

From Humble Beginnings to Worldwide Fame

For basketball fans, spring is one of the most exciting times of the year. In March, college basketball teams from across the United States compete in a popular and exciting playoff tournament that is commonly known as March Madness. Later in spring, the excitement picks up again with the National Basketball Association (NBA) playoffs. During these action-packed months, basketball enthusiasts spend time and money to celebrate their favorite teams and watch them on the road to the final championship game. Long-time Boston Celtics fan Nick Abisi traveled almost 1,000 miles (1,600 km) from his home in Indianapolis, Indiana, to celebrate in Boston, Massachusetts, when his favorite team won the NBA championship in 2008. "This is not a team; it's a way of life,"[1] he said. Many basketball fans would certainly agree with Abisi; caring about their team is a huge part of their lives.

Basketball was not always this popular, however. It had humble beginnings before growing to become one of the most popular sports in the United States and a growing sport around the world. A physical education teacher named James Naismith was looking for a new game to entertain his young male students at a school in Springfield, Massachusetts. The boys were tired of the usual exercises, such as jumping jacks, sit-ups, push-ups, and gymnastics, and Naismith later recalled, "The invention of basketball was not an accident. It was developed to meet a need."[2] When Naismith tacked two peach baskets to the walls of the gym at the Young Men's Christian Association (YMCA) International Training School, which was also known as the School for Christian Workers, he had no idea how popular his new game would become.

Basketball might not involve actual baskets anymore, but many of Naismith's original ideas for the sport have remained for more than 100 years. As the sport has evolved, so has the understanding of the science behind it. From its earliest days, science has played an important part in every basketball game, and knowledge of the scientific factors at play in the sport have allowed for rule changes, equipment changes, and other improvements that have pushed the sport further than Naismith himself could have ever dreamed.

An All-American Sport

It is hard to imagine a time before basketball was played on courts across the United States, but before 1891, basketball did not exist. It was only created after Naismith's superiors asked him to create a new game to help the young men at the school get through the long Massachusetts winter. Naismith wanted to come up with something that was interesting, easy to learn, and safe to play indoors. It was also important to him that the game involve skill and scientific thinking. He said, "It is our place to encourage games that may be played by gentlemen in a manly way, and show them that science is superior to brute force."[3]

Naismith decided to review other games that were popular at the time, including rugby, soccer, and lacrosse. All of these games involved two teams moving a ball back and forth on a field or court to get it to a goal. Naismith decided his game would be similar. To eliminate unnecessary pushing and tackling to get the ball into the goals, which would pose problems indoors, he decided to place the goals above head height. Placing the goals above players' heads would also keep them from preventing teams from scoring simply by standing in front of them, and it encouraged players to develop a new skill set instead of relying only on physical strength.

At Naismith's request, the gym's janitor searched for boxes that could be used as goals. He found two peach baskets. They would do, Naismith decided. An elevated railing formed a gallery 10 feet (3 m) above the gym floor, and a basket was nailed to the railing at each end. With the baskets in place, the game of basketball was born—the first major sport born in the United States.

This example of the peach baskets used in early basketball games can be found at the Naismith Memorial Basketball Hall of Fame in Springfield.

Fast Break!

Basketball is considered an American sport, but James Naismith was born in Ontario, Canada.

A Slamming Success

With the baskets and a ball (originally a soccer ball) in place, Naismith sat down to create the rules of the game. The ball could not be bounced, he decided. It could only be passed from player to player. There could be no walking or running with the ball. The player had to throw it from the spot where he caught it. A point would be scored each time the ball went into the basket and stayed there. Rough play such as pushing, tripping, or holding an opponent would count as a foul. An umpire would ensure fair play. The game would be short—just 30 minutes with a 5-minute rest break between 15-minute halves—with no limit on the size of the team. "The more players, the more fun,"[4] Naismith decided.

Naismith's game was an instant hit with his class, who did not care that they had to climb up and remove the ball from the basket whenever a point was scored because the baskets still had a bottom. They took the idea home with them on Christmas vacation and taught their friends to play. When they returned, they organized teams to play against each other. Spectators and crowds began gathering to watch the enthusiastic competitions. Naismith was asked to make copies of the rules, and they were soon published in the school newspaper.

As word of the game got around, physical education teacher Senda Berenson Abbott introduced it to her female students at Smith College in nearby Northampton, Massachusetts. Her first teams hit the court in 1892. The game caught on and quickly spread from Smith to other women's colleges across the country. Many people were afraid that female basketball players would not be strong enough to play the game, because women were seen as the weaker sex at the time. That was not the case, however. Senda Berenson Abbott wrote, "The game … has been encouraged because by means of it the girls have been made strong and agile in body, keen and fearless in mind, and unselfish and loyal in spirit."[5] Basketball helped young women grow stronger mentally and physically, and it taught them to work together as teammates.

Fast Break!

Clara Gregory Baer published the first set of women's basketball rules in 1895.

Women have been playing basketball since the sport's earliest days.

The Red Heads Go Pro

The All American Red Heads were one of the first professional women's basketball teams in the United States. They were established in 1936, played until 1986, and remain the longest-running women's professional basketball team. They were considered a barnstorming team, much like today's Harlem Globetrotters. Barnstorming teams travel to various locations to play sports, even though they are not part of an established league.

The Red Heads were founded by C. M. Olson, and their name was inspired by Olson's wife, who owned a number of beauty salons. Fans throughout the years loved the Red Heads because of their impressive play, which included trick shots and skills such as dribbling with their knees. The Red Heads would play against men's teams across the country, and they won more often than they lost. Although the team disbanded in 1986, in 2012, the Red Heads were inducted into the Naismith Memorial Basketball Hall of Fame as the first women's team to achieve that high honor.

Improvements and Updates

As with all new inventions, basketball needed a few changes and improvements to make it work better. The peach baskets were replaced with wire and mesh hoops, and eventually, the hole at the bottom of the basket—also known as the net—was created to allow the ball to fall through it and back onto the court. Backboards were installed to keep spectators in the balconies from interfering with the basket. Team size was set at five players on each side to prevent overcrowding on the court. Later, team numbers were expanded to include 10 to 15 players, but a limit of 5 per team on the court at a given time remained the rule.

New terms such as "blocking" and "charging" then came into use. Blocking is legally hitting or catching a ball that is being shot toward the basket without touching the opponent's hands. Charging is creating illegal contact by moving or pushing into an opponent's body. Running with the ball—now known as "traveling" and originally considered a foul—became a violation, meaning that the only penalty was loss of possession.

Dribbling—controlling or advancing the ball by bouncing it—was introduced early in the game but quickly became a cause for dispute. Naismith's rules stated that the ball had to be thrown from the place where it was caught. Ingenious players tried to get around this, however, with moves such as tapping the ball into the air, taking a step and then catching it. Some rolled it, ran after it, and picked it up. Others simply bounced it. Such moves were frowned upon by traditionalists, but dribbling continued and was quickly accepted in women's and collegiate games. Then, players began to develop specific dribbling skills such as the "behind the back," the "crossover," and the "half-reverse" dribble. In the crossover, the player dribbles one-handed, then abruptly changes hands and dribbles one-handed in another direction. In the half-reverse, the player turns, pretending to be reversing direction, then turns back and dribbles in the original direction.

Barnstorming Becomes Popular

Basketball was first introduced and played in YMCAs, and therefore, many YMCA teams were the first to turn professional and charge spectators to watch their games. These games were often held in large halls because the YMCA gyms had grown too small to host the events.

In 1897, 12 amateur teams met to take part in the Amateur Athletic Union's (AAU's) first national basketball championship tournament. After winning the tournament, the 23rd Street YMCA team from New York City decided to go professional, but professional athletes had a bad reputation at the time. Early physical education instructor Luther Halsey Gulick wrote, "When men commence to make money out of sport, it degenerates with most tremendous speed ... It has in the past inevitably resulted in men of lower character going into the game."[6]

Without a home court, the 23rd Street team changed its name to the New York Wanderers and gained fame as the first basketball barnstormers. The term "barnstormer" was initially used to describe stunt pilots who traveled to rural parts of the country, landed at local farms, and put on air shows for area residents. Basketball barnstormers such as the Wanderers and the Troy Trojans toured small and large towns by bus and train, played one or two games for pay, and then moved on. They had no contracts and no guarantees. Pay was so low that many players had to work at other jobs to survive. Some played for more than one team at a time. Their schedule involved hours of travel interrupted by hotly contested games in school gyms, armories (military structures), and meeting halls.

During this time, the first professional basketball league was formed in the United States. The National Basketball League was created in 1898 and featured teams from the northeastern United States. Although it only lasted until 1903, this league paved the way for the NBA.

From Black Barnstormers to Integrated Leagues

By the 1920s, there were hundreds of men's professional basketball teams. All were independent, and like the rest of American society at the time, all were segregated by race. Nevertheless, dozens of talented African American men played on amateur and professional teams sponsored by black churches, social clubs, businesses, colleges, and YMCAs. Such all-black teams were known as "Black Fives," for the number of players per team.

Two Black Five barnstorming teams—the New York Renaissance, also known as the Harlem Rens, and the Harlem Globetrotters—quickly made names for themselves as the best in the business. The Rens played for more than 25 years and had a win-loss record of 2,588–529. Many of their wins were against top all-white teams, such as the Original Celtics. The Globetrotters, originally known as the Savoy Big Five, began barnstorming in 1927, played as many as 175 games a year, and won more than 90 percent of them at their peak of success. By 1949, thanks to their uniquely entertaining skills, they were basketball's most popular team. The Globetrotters continue to pack arenas thanks to the skills that first helped them stand out in the early days of the sport: "spinning the ball on a fingertip … fancy dribbling, trick shooting, and comedy routines."[7]

The Harlem Globetrotters are not part of the NBA, but they still travel around the United States, entertaining audiences with their impressive skills that seem to defy the laws of physics.

Despite both teams' immense popularity, their travel schedules were regularly complicated by the fact that they were not welcome in most restaurants and hotels because they were black. However, beginning in the late 1940s, integration began to change basketball. The NBA formed in 1949 as North America's top professional basketball league, and in 1950, Chuck Cooper became the first African American drafted by the NBA. By the 1960s, African Americans were highly visible on both college and professional basketball teams. The percentage of black NBA players continued to grow throughout the years. In 2015, nearly 75 percent of all NBA players were black.

The Rise of College Basketball

At the same time that professional basketball developed, high school and college teams grew as well. Only a few good players were needed to make a team, so even small schools could be competitive and could generate positive attention through the sport.

The first official intercollegiate game using five-player teams was played in January 1896, when the University of Chicago defeated the University of Iowa by a score of 15–12. In April of that same year, the first intercollegiate women's basketball game was played between Stanford University and the University of California, Berkeley. Stanford won that game 2–1.

The National Collegiate Athletic Association (NCAA) was created and sponsored its first national tournament in 1939, but a large number of college leagues that developed were regional. The NCAA Division I Men's Basketball Tournament, which is the official name for today's March Madness, did not draw a national audience until the rise of television in the 1950s.

A remarkable group of college athletes in the 1950s and 1960s also helped college basketball gain popularity during this time. Players such as Elgin Baylor, Oscar Robertson, Wilt Chamberlain, and Bill Russell became stars, defying earlier basketball customs and creating new plays such as the head fake, the running bank shot, and the fadeaway jump shot. The head fake involves a player moving their head to make it look as though they are going in one direction before actually moving in another direction. A running bank shot is a shot made when a running player bounces the ball off the backboard and into the basket. A fadeaway jump shot is a shot taken while the player is jumping backward away from the basket.

Fans were amazed by their heroes' size and agility. Baylor and Robertson were 6 feet 5 inches (2 m) tall, Russell was 6 feet 10 inches (2.1 m) tall, and Chamberlain was 7 feet 1 inch (2.2 m) tall. When those men went on to become professional players, other exceptional college athletes took their place. In the 1970s and 1980s, teams such as the University of California, Los Angeles (UCLA) Bruins, the University of North Carolina (UNC) Tar Heels, and the Indiana Hoosiers (Indiana University) became known for producing star players such as Kareem Abdul-Jabbar, Michael Jordan, and Larry Bird.

College basketball players continue to captivate fans. Superstar NBA players such as Stephen Curry, Chris Paul, and Dwyane Wade all made names for themselves as collegiate athletes first. Today's best female basketball players, including Maya Moore, Elena Delle Donne, Skylar Diggins, and Diana Taurasi, also became famous during their years in college.

College basketball games allow fans to see future stars of the sport in action.

From Title IX to Title Games

Although women's basketball programs in U.S. colleges had existed since the sport's earliest days, it took until 1972 for those teams to be placed on equal footing with their male counterparts in terms of the law. That year, a law was passed requiring that schools receiving money from the federal government give girls and women the same opportunities to play sports as boys and men. This law, which is called Title IX or Title Nine, helped women's sports grow in a major way.

In the years since Title IX was passed, many collegiate teams have risen to national fame, but one program stands out above the rest, especially in recent years: the University of Connecticut (UConn) Huskies. This team, which has been coached by Geno Auriemma since 1985, holds many college basketball records, including a record 111-game winning streak that lasted from 2014 to 2017. The Huskies have also won 11 NCAA women's championships as of 2017, including four in a row from 2013 to 2016.

UConn is known as one of the top colleges in the country for female basketball players. Many of the best professional women's basketball players attended this school.

Going Pro

When it was founded in 1949, the NBA was made up of 17 professional basketball teams. As of 2017, it is made up of 30 teams, almost doubling in size in less than 70 years. The NBA-backed Women's National Basketball Association (WNBA) began playing games in 1997. Although the WNBA has been around for decades and has many passionate fans, it is still nowhere near as popular as the NBA. However, as Val Ackerman, the first WNBA president said, "Longevity is itself a victory. There were naysayers around every corner who said we wouldn't last a year or even two years, and now it's 20."[8]

Stephen Curry is one example of a star basketball player who has used science to excel in the NBA.

In the 21st century, Naismith's game is played professionally in more than 200 countries around the world. The International Basketball Federation (FIBA), founded in 1932 in Geneva, Switzerland, includes a total of 214 national member federations. World championship tournaments for men and women, known as World Cups, take place every four years, and the champion wins the Naismith Trophy, named in honor of basketball's creator.

In the United States, basketball is a national passion, with media and fans unable to get enough of the feats of players such as Curry, LeBron James, and Kevin Durant. They are constantly in the news, and young players aspire to walk in their shoes. Their popularity has also led the sport to become highly commercialized, with television networks and advertisers paying millions of dollars to secure broadcasting rights and advertising deals and players signing profitable NBA contracts.

With so much fame and fortune at stake, competition to get to the top in the sport is fierce, and aspiring players and their coaches know that height and natural talent is no longer enough to succeed. Knowing this, most turn to science to improve their performance. A deeper understanding of science allows players and coaches to train hard, prevent and treat injuries correctly, and excel on the court. The greatest players in the sport did not get there by accident or through luck and raw skill alone; they needed science to help them become the best they could be.

Chapter 2

Training for Results

When basketball was just beginning, it was a sport played for fun and recreation, and as a result, players did not study the science behind training techniques or the skills they displayed on the court. Many athletes relied on what they knew: Eat healthy, get plenty of sleep, and try your best on the court. They used simply their natural athletic abilities to carry out the moves of the game.

Since then, science and the sport have progressed, and people discovered that when players followed a training plan, kept themselves in peak physical condition, and used scientific knowledge to prepare their body for athletic competition, they became even faster, stronger, and more agile. Athletic training has become a serious business that employs thousands of people across the world and keeps players busy all year. "It's a year-round job," said Steven M. Traina, a physician for the NBA's Denver Nuggets. "Most of our players have been working out together prior to [training] camp, having informal workouts. Guys just don't go fishing and then show up and play basketball."[9]

Training can be tough on an athlete's body, but a strong understanding of science helps basketball players know how hard they can push themselves in their workouts without going too far and causing injuries. Every sprint, stretch, and weightlifting session involves many body systems working together, and learning how to make them work together in a healthy and productive way is one of the keys to success on the basketball court.

Making Muscles Healthy and Strong

Basketball players need strength, speed, and agility to play the game well, and that calls for healthy muscles. The human body is made up of three types of muscles: smooth muscle in the blood vessels and body organs; cardiac muscle in the walls of the heart; and skeletal muscle, which produces movement and supports the skeleton.

Skeletal muscles can be controlled consciously, which is what allows the body to move the way a person wants or needs it to. There are more than 600 skeletal muscles in the human body. Skeletal muscles are made up of bundles of individual cells called "myocytes." These are also known as muscle fibers. Found within each cell are myofibrils, which are long strands of protein that lengthen and shorten. When they shorten, the muscle contracts (becomes shorter and thicker) and moves the body part it is attached to.

Muscle fibers are also divided into different types depending on how fast they contract. Slow-twitch fibers contract slowly, with little force for long periods of time. Fast-twitch fibers contract quickly and powerfully and tire rapidly. The human body is generally made up of both types of muscle fibers, but some individuals have more of one type than another. Marathon runners, for instance, can have up to 80 percent slow-twitch fibers, which help them run for hours on end. The muscles of sprinters, on the other hand, are sometimes made up of 80 percent fast-twitch fibers, which are needed for short, powerful bursts of speed.

Basketball players practice sprints to help strengthen their fast-twitch muscle fibers.

Basketball is a game that requires both endurance and bursts of energy, so players work to develop both their fast-twitch and slow-twitch muscle fibers. To develop fast-twitch fibers, they practice jumping or sprinting. For slow-twitch fibers, they focus on endurance workouts. They swim or tread water, jog, or lift relatively light hand weights for long periods of time.

Harder, Faster, Stronger

Fast-twitch muscles help basketball players because they need to be quick on the court. To work on speed, they practice sprints and other drills, such as line jumps (jumping quickly back and forth over a line), running backward, and jumping rope rapidly. However, speed is not the only quality good basketball players need to have. They must also be strong and agile.

Strength is essential for basketball players because they need strong muscles to jump, throw, and guard other players. The more often their muscles contract against resistance, the stronger they get. As muscles are pushed to the point of fatigue during workouts that emphasize muscle contraction, new cells repair the muscles. This increases the thickness of muscle fibers and makes the muscles stronger. Basketball players build strength by using exercise equipment such as free weights, weight machines, and medicine balls. They repeat sets of squats and lunges to build strength in their leg muscles, as

Dealing With DOMS

Athletes and other people who exercise often feel soreness in their muscles 24 to 72 hours after working out, especially after beginning a new exercise or training program. The scientific name for this condition is Delayed Onset Muscle Soreness (DOMS), and scientists are continuing to study its complex causes.

For years, researchers thought DOMS resulted from increased lactic acid concentrations in the muscles. Studies, however, proved that high levels of lactic acid do not remain in the muscles long after exercise. Today, many experts believe the pain is a result of microscopic tearing of muscle fibers brought on by exercise.

There is no magical cure for DOMS. Gentle stretching, warming up, and cooling down before and after exercise may reduce its severity. Ice packs, over-the-counter pain relievers, and massage therapy can also be used to treat muscle soreness.

well as bicep curls, bench presses, and push-ups to build strength in the muscles of their upper body. No muscle group is overlooked. Dribbling, for instance, requires a great deal of finger and wrist strength, so players work this specific area by doing forearm curls with a pair of hand weights.

In the past, people believed that having too much muscle mass would negatively affect a player's ability to shoot the ball and move easily down the court. However, as Traina has said, this attitude has changed over the years: "People used to think in basketball that if you lifted weights, you couldn't shoot because you'd be too muscle-bound ... [Players] spend a lot of time in the weight room. You look at the athletes now compared to 20 or 25 years ago, and they're cut, they're muscular."[10]

Basketball players need to be strong, but they need to learn how to move their muscular bodies with agility, which is the ability to move quickly, smoothly, and with good coordination and balance. To improve agility, players focus on drills that involve rapid weaving, sprinting, and shuffling in complex patterns. These include drills in which they sprint around cones set in staggered patterns. They also do side-to-side jumping drills to help with lateral, or sideways, mobility.

These drills help players develop a strong sense of proprioception, which is an awareness of the body in space. Athletes with good proprioception are aware of the placement of their limbs without needing to look at them, which is helpful for basketball players who need to run quickly down the court and change direction while still looking ahead instead of at their feet. Sensors called proprioceptors in muscles, tendons, and joints send messages to the brain about their position, which allows the athlete to maintain their balance and coordination without using their eyes to check on the position of their feet. Repetitive drills such as the ones listed above help basketball players improve their proprioception, which enhances their agility.

Fast Break!

NBA players run for an average distance of approximately 2.5 miles (4 km) per game.

Instinct Through Training

Agility is best showcased when movements are performed instinctively. To make basketball moves automatic, players work to develop muscle memory. Muscle memory is the ability of the brain to remember and direct the body to carry out often-repeated muscle moves without conscious thinking.

Shooting a basketball involves muscle memory. Former coach Jerry Tarkanian said, "Like practically everything else in life, basketball shooting is a habitual thing; that is, it involves repetition of a given set of movements until those movements become an unconscious part

Players practice shooting over and over so they can take a shot during a game without thinking about its mechanics and instead can focus on things such as avoiding defenders or checking the shot clock.

of a player's court behavior."[11] For average people, movements such as walking are controlled by muscle memory; they don't have to think about the act of walking while they are doing it because they have repeated the movement so many times. For elite athletes, much more difficult skills, such as shooting a jump shot and executing a crossover dribble, become as automatic as walking.

It has been estimated that the average athlete must repeat a complex move such as shooting the basketball correctly about 20,000 times to commit it to muscle memory. Because basketball players execute moves they would not ordinarily do in life, such as running backward and dribbling while changing direction, they have to practice for hundreds of hours until moves become unconscious. NBA legend Bill Russell, who was renowned for his defense and shot-blocking skills during his time in the league, stated,

> *Defense is a science … not a … thing you just luck into. Every move has six or seven years of work behind it. In basketball your body gets to do things it couldn't do in normal circumstances. You take abnormal steps, you have to run backward almost as fast as you can run forward. On defense you must never cross your legs while*

running, and that's the most natural thing to do when changing direction. Instead, you try to glide like a crab. You have to fight the natural tendencies and do things naturally that aren't natural.[12]

Fast Break!

The current record holder for most three-point shots made in a season, Stephen Curry, takes as many as 2,000 practice shots each week.

Plyometric Drills

Basketball players need bursts of power to execute jump shots, rebounds, passes, and other moves. Plyometric drills, designed to generate fast, explosive movements, help them increase their power. These drills quickly stretch and contract muscles, exerting maximum force in short intervals of time. Stretching makes muscles longer, and contracting shortens them. Doing exercises that stretch and contract muscles increases muscle power and speed. Plyometric drills also improve the function of the central nervous system. Repeated drills condition nerves to improve reaction time, causing a fast, powerful contraction of muscles. The concept was developed in the 1960s by Soviet scientist Yuri Verkhoshansky, who called it "shock training." U.S. track and field coach Fred Wilt coined the term "plyometrics" in 1975.

Plyometric drills are fast and strenuous. For example, during clap push-ups, athletes first get into a push-up position. They then repeatedly push up, clap their hands together, then quickly put their hands down to catch themselves. To execute power skips, athletes drive their knees forcefully upward as they skip forward. The arms are moved in a forceful, exaggerated running motion.

Amazing Ambidexterity

Ambidexterity is the ability to use either hand with ease for different activities, and it is unusual in everyday life. Most people are right-handed. That means they are more skillful using their right hand than their left. Studies suggest that 70 to 90 percent of the world's population is right-handed.

Ambidexterity is an asset in basketball. Players who can use both their right and left hands for dribbling and shooting have a definite advantage over single-hand-dominant players. Therefore, many players train for hours to be able to use either hand. Such has been the case with Stephen Curry, LeBron James, and Kobe Bryant. Forwards Michael Beasley of the NBA's Miami Heat and Candace Parker of the WNBA's Los Angeles Sparks are both naturally ambidextrous.

Plyometric training can be especially effective for basketball players because of its impact on an athlete's vertical jump. Basketball players need to achieve a good height on their vertical jump to shoot the ball, block shots, rebound, and slam dunk. Because jumps are such a basic component of plyometric training regimens, it has been noted that plyometrics can

improve an athlete's vertical jump. According to a 2007 scientific study, "PT [plyometric training] significantly improves vertical jump height in all four types of standard vertical jumps ... From this perspective, PT can be recommended as an effective form of physical conditioning for augmenting the vertical jump performance of healthy individuals."[13]

Plyometric training is used to help basketball players get the height they need to execute a perfect slam dunk.

Eating Well to Play Well

Exercise is one way basketball players stay in game shape; eating the right foods is another. Athletes need to fuel their body properly to get the best results out of their training and to perform at their highest level in games. The best way to achieve this is to eat a variety of nutritious foods that include fruits, vegetables, lean meats, and whole grains. All of these food groups provide the strength and energy needed to play basketball.

It may seem as though professional athletes eat a restricted diet, but they just eat a healthy one. They actually take in more calories than an average person because their body needs more fuel to power all the physical activity they do. In contrast to the average person, who needs about 2,000 calories per day to carry out routine tasks, a male basketball player who is 7 feet (2.1 m) tall may need up to 7,000 calories per day. A calorie is a measure of the energy found in food. An egg has between 70 and 80 calories. A banana has around 100 calories. A piece of chocolate cake has more than 200 calories.

It is important for basketball players to eat healthy foods that will give them energy and be used to keep their body strong and fit. Carbohydrates provide energy needed for physical activity and are found in whole grains, fruits, vegetables, beans, and potatoes. Processed sugars such as those found in candy and soda are also carbohydrates, but they do not provide long-lasting energy. Athletes limit their intake of processed sugars. Proteins are building blocks needed to make muscles and virtually every other body tissue. They make up enzymes, which power many chemical reactions, and hemoglobin, which carries oxygen in the blood. The body cannot store protein, so players need to eat it to ensure there is always a supply of it in their body. Sources of protein eaten by athletes include chicken, fish, cheese, nuts, and eggs. Fats should be limited to heart-healthy oils such as sunflower or olive oil.

Drinking plenty of water or low-sugar sports drinks is also important for players to maintain healthy body systems. Fluid is important for regulating temperature through sweating, eliminating waste products, and facilitating digestion. Even a loss of 2 percent of one's body weight through sweating can cause a drop in blood volume. When that happens, the heart has to work harder to move blood through the body. Dehydrated players do not have enough fluid in their body, and they may experience muscle cramps, dizziness, fatigue, or even heat exhaustion or heat stroke.

Dehydration can negatively affect an athlete's performance, so it is important for basketball players to drink small amounts of fluid throughout training sessions and games.

What's on the Menu?

Basketball players in training eat a diet high in carbohydrates and lean proteins and low in fats, simple sugars, and alcohol. The following is an example of Cleveland Cavaliers guard Iman Shumpert's daily diet:

For breakfast:

• An [omelet], usually ham bacon cheese with spinach in it
• A fruit smoothie with any type of vegetables in the house: kale, salad, broccoli, carrots ...

Lunch:

• Salad with cheese, boiled egg chopped up, mixed in with kale
• Bowl of fruit
• Cold cut sandwich or soup ...

After practice:

• Turkey or chicken

Early dinner:

• "When I get home around 4 or 5, I eat something heavier. Steak, pasta anything like that."

Second dinner:

• "At night ... around 8–9, I'll eat again ... it will be a salmon or a cold cut anything light or chicken [C]aesar salad."[1]

The diet of Iman Shumpert, shown here, includes protein for building muscles, as well as carbohydrates for energy.

1. Quoted in Nina Mandell, "How to Eat Like an NBA Player, According to Cavaliers Guard Iman Shumpert," *USA Today*, November 6, 2015. ftw.usatoday.com/2015/11/how-to-eat-like-an-nba-player-according-to-cavaliers-guard-iman-shumpert.

In Addition to Nutrition

When training and good nutrition is not enough, some basketball players turn to supplements to improve their performance on the court. A few supplements, such as high-protein drinks and vitamins, are considered acceptable within sports associations, including the NBA, WNBA, and NCAA, because they are made of naturally-occurring ingredients. Creatine, a supplement that allegedly builds muscles and generates energy, is a legal and popular supplement, but schools are not allowed to provide creatine to their athletes because its safety has not been proven and it gives athletes who use it an unfair advantage over those who do not.

Many performance-enhancing substances are banned by all sports organizations in the United States. These include stimulants such as cocaine

Joakim Noah believed taking a banned substance would help him recover more quickly from an injury. Instead, it led to a suspension.

and amphetamines, narcotics such as heroin and morphine, cannabinoids such as marijuana, hormones such as human growth hormone (HGH), and anabolic steroids. Anabolic steroids are synthetically produced variants of the male hormone testosterone. Like testosterone, they increase muscle size and strength and improve a player's stamina, but they do not occur naturally in the body.

In March 2017, New York Knicks player Joakim Noah received a 20-game suspension for taking a banned muscle-building supplement. In a statement, Noah revealed that he had taken the banned substance to help him return to playing shape after an injury:

> *"I tried to take a supplement to help me with everything that I was going through," Noah said, intimating that he took it while rehabbing from a hamstring injury he suffered in early February. "I've gone through a lot of injuries and I tried to take something to help me and it backfired."*[14]

A number of professional athletes have turned to steroids or other performance-enhancing drugs to help them as they train to come back from an injury. They believe these drugs will help them regain the strength they need to revive their career. However, these substances are banned for a reason, and they can be dangerous.

Not Worth the Risk

Some people argue that most basketball players are unlikely to use steroids because they do not want to pack on weight and muscle mass. Instead, they want to be lean, agile, and quick. Still, there are banned substances other than steroids, and a number of players have been caught and fined for using them. In 2016, Milwaukee Bucks player O. J. Mayo was banned from the NBA for violating its substance abuse policy by taking an undisclosed "drug of abuse." According to the sports news website Deadspin,

> *The NBA's list of drugs of abuse includes:*
>
> - *Amphetamine and its analogs (including, but not limited to, methamphetamine and MDMA)*
> - *Cocaine*
> - *LSD*
> - *Opiates (Heroin, Codeine, Morphine)*
> - *Phencyclidine (PCP)*[15]

Mayo will be eligible for reinstatement in 2018.

Substance abuse is potentially a more serious problem among teen basketball players who are just getting into the game and think that steroids will help them qualify for sports scholarships or

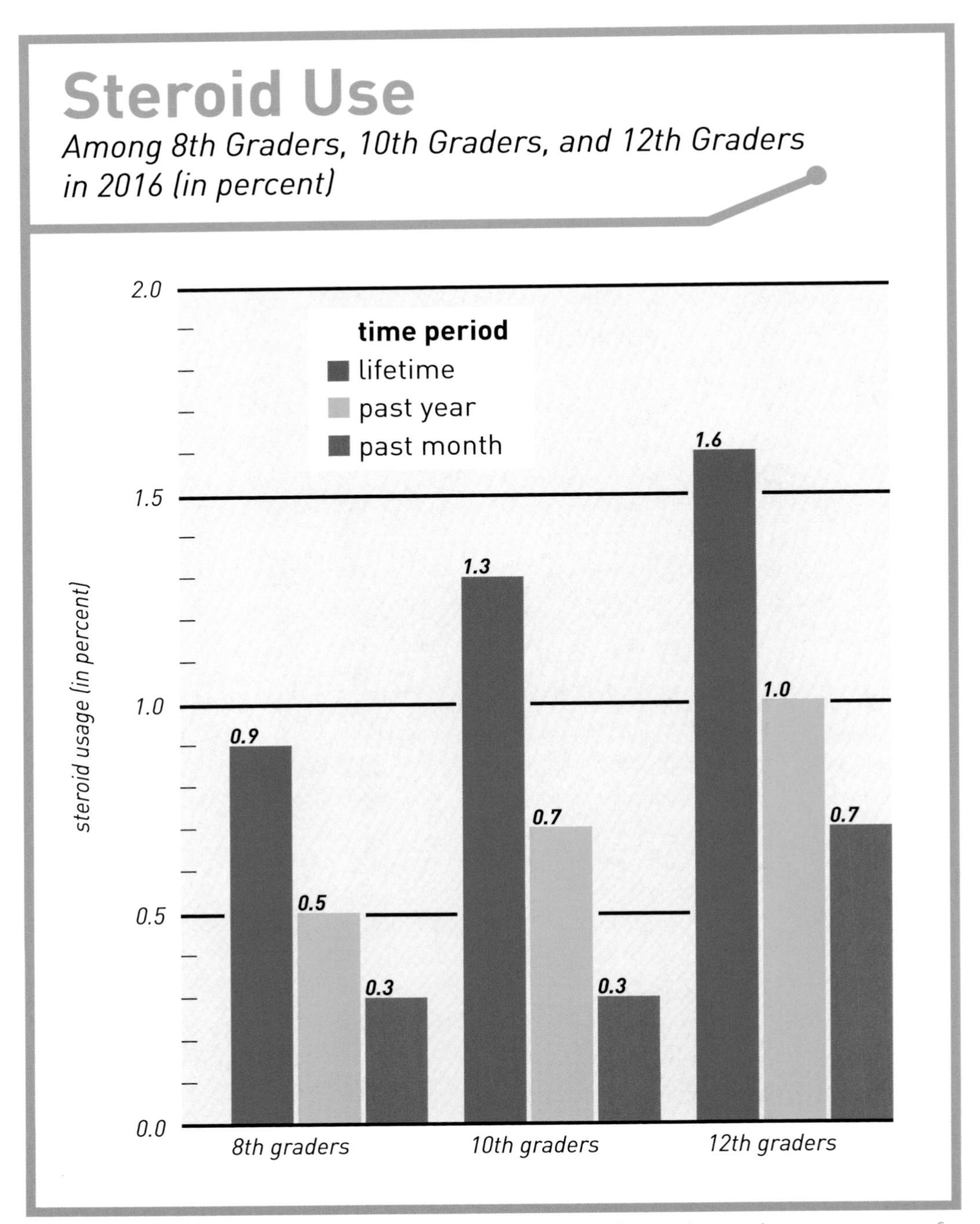

This information from the National Institute on Drug Abuse shows the percentage of U.S. students who used steroids in 2016.

lead to professional careers. According to the National Institute on Drug Abuse, 1.6 percent of 12th graders have used steroids at some point in their lifetime as of 2016. This is despite the fact that steroids can have serious side effects such as high blood pressure, liver damage, and stunted growth. Dr. Gary Wadler, an expert on steroid abuse, explained the unique risks to young adults who are still growing: "What happens is that steroids close the growth centers in a kid's bones. Once these growth plates are closed, they cannot reopen so adolescents that take too many steroids may end up shorter than they should have been."[16]

Due to the fact that steroids and other performance-enhancing drugs have so many dangerous side effects, experts believe that everyone—from teens to professionals—should realize that they can become great athletes without drugs. It is more difficult to convince professional or collegiate athletes of this after they have been injured, but with proper treatment and better understanding of injuries, basketball players can return to the court without resorting to performance-enhancing drugs.

Chapter 3

Injuries: Sidelining Star Athletes

Every athlete's worst nightmare is getting seriously injured, and despite all of the precautions taken during training, sometimes injuries happen. In basketball, especially, this is not surprising because players do not wear any protective gear or padding. Players' joints and muscles pull and twist as they pivot, jump, and sprint down the court. Sometimes, players also run into each other, trip and fall, or get hit accidentally by other players. As NBA.com writer Dan Bell has stated,

> *The physically demanding nature of NBA basketball requires a fine-tuned body capable of surviving 82-plus games each year. But bumps, bruises and, unfortunately, injuries are always a part of each season. Staying healthy and, where necessary, coming back as quickly as possible from an injury, are vital to any team's success.*[17]

Injuries are part of the game, and they can be scary, especially for basketball players who have never been hurt before. However, scientific knowledge of why injuries occur and how they can be treated is constantly improving, and this knowledge is a huge asset for basketball players as they work to avoid getting hurt or get back on the court quickly after being sidelined by an injury.

Is It Broken?

Basketball injuries fall into two general categories: acute and chronic. Chronic injuries—also known as overuse injuries—develop over time, whereas acute injuries are caused by specific events such as a forceful hit, hard falls, or unnatural movements. Depending on the severity of the acute injury, such events can lead to pain, swelling, dislocated joints, broken bones, or even loss of consciousness.

Broken bones are some of the most common acute injuries, especially for basketball players. A break can be as simple as a tiny crack in a bone or as complicated as a compound fracture, in which the bone is completely broken and punctures the skin. Depending on the severity and location of the break, team doctors sometimes use splints and tape to brace and protect the injury to allow a player to continue to participate in practices and games. This often happens with small fractures in fingers. In other cases, the player must sit out of the game for weeks or months until the break has time to heal. Bad breaks sometimes require surgery and the placement of rods, pins, or screws in the body to reset the bone.

Jammed, sprained, or broken fingers are common basketball injuries because players have to catch a hard ball traveling quickly and with a lot of force. A splint is sometimes used to protect an injured finger while an athlete continues playing.

Another common acute injury is a contusion, commonly called a bruise, which happens when a body part hits or is hit by a hard object, such as a basketball, the floor of the court, or a body part of another player. A bruise is an area where small blood vessels known as capillaries have been damaged, allowing blood to leak out and accumulate in the surrounding tissue. This causes a reddish-purple mark that slowly changes color over time. Although most bruises are not severe, some can be dangerous. A hard blow that bruises an organ can cause permanent damage. Bruises on the brain can lead to swelling, concussion, coma, and in severe cases, even death.

"I Literally Almost Threw Up"

Compound fractures are not common basketball injuries, so when they occur, they frighten everyone who sees the bone sticking out of the skin. This was especially true in March 2013, when Louisville's Kevin Ware sustained a compound fracture in his lower right leg—the bone breaking in two pieces—during a game against Duke University in the NCAA Midwest Region final, which is part of the nationally televised March Madness tournament.

The injury and the reaction to it were described in the *New York Times*:

> *The [Louisville] Cardinals led by 21–17 when Duke's Tyler Thornton broke free for a 3-point jump shot from the right wing. Ware dashed from*

Kevin Ware, shown here during his time playing college basketball in Georgia after his injury, trained long and hard to get back into playing shape following his fracture.

1. Pat Brozi, "An Innocuous Play, a Gruesome Injury," New York Times, March 31, 2013. www.nytimes.com/2013/04/01/sports/ncaabasketball/kevin-wares-gruesome-injury-shakes-and-rallies-louisville.html?_r=0.

the edge of the foul circle and jumped at Thornton to try to block the shot. Spinning in the air, Ware landed with all his weight on his right leg. The lower part of his leg buckled unnaturally, and he slid into the Louisville bench. He lay on his back with the lower leg dangling grotesquely, broken at the middle of the shin ...

[Louisville coach Rick] Pitino said a broken bone punctured the skin. "I went over and was going to help him up, and then all of a sudden I saw what it was," he said. "And I literally almost threw up. And then I just wanted to get a towel to get it over that."[1]

Ware was immediately taken to the hospital to have surgery, because this kind of injury can be deadly if left untreated for too long. He had surgery to reset the bone and place a rod in his leg. The surgery was successful, and Ware was with his teammates—but still unable to play—when they won the NCAA championship only a couple of weeks later.

Sprains and Strains, Twists and Turns

Strains and sprains are two other common acute injuries. Strains involve stretched or torn tendons—the tissues that connect muscles to bones—or muscles. They can occur anywhere, but they are most common in the back, the hamstrings (muscles at the back of the leg—from the thigh to the knee), and the elbows. Sprains occur when ligaments—the tough, fibrous tissues that connect bones to other bones—are overstretched or torn.

Because basketball players are always making sharp turns and twists, sprained ankles are the most common type of sprain in basketball. Most sprained ankles are lateral sprains involving the anterior talofibular ligament on the outside of the ankle. Players damage this ligament when the ankle rolls onto the outside part of the foot.

A high ankle sprain is rarer but more serious than a lateral sprain. High sprains often occur when the foot is forced to rotate outward or when the foot cannot move and the leg is twisted. Damage is done to the syndesmotic ligaments, which lie above the ankle joint and wrap around the lower part of the shin. When these ligaments tear, the two bones may separate when a player puts weight on the foot. The injury results in an unstable ankle, which is extremely painful. The patient may have to wear a cast and take up to six weeks to recover. In some cases, surgery is required, and the recovery time for such a severe sprain could be as long as six months.

Fast Break!

A major study of sports injuries conducted in 2009 showed that more than 500,000 basketball-related injuries were treated in U.S. emergency rooms that year.

Out of Place

Dislocations are another type of acute injury common to basketball. In a dislocation, a force moves bones from their normal position in a joint. Bones are commonly held in place by ligaments, tendons, and muscles, so these are all injured during a dislocation.

Finger joints are delicate and easily dislocated by a fall or other impact. The most common finger dislocations occur in the middle knuckle of fingers. This often occurs when a finger gets jammed when a player catches the ball or falls on the floor. In February 2016, Kobe Bryant of the Los Angeles Lakers dislocated his middle finger while catching himself after slipping on the floor. Bryant said, "I couldn't spread my palm fast enough, so my finger just jammed right into the floor and it just popped right out."[18] Bryant then had a trainer pop the finger back into place, so he could keep playing. In some cases, this can be done for dislocations, but further treatment and tests to see if any other injuries occurred with the dislocation are often required.

Fast Break!

A human hand is made up of 27 bones.

Shoulders can dislocate, too, when a hard impact causes the rounded head of the upper arm bone to pop out of the socket. Dislocations of most joints are relatively easy to fix by manipulating the joint until the two bones are properly aligned again, but rest and protection of the injured area are necessary for a full recovery to be made.

Knee Injuries

Players sometimes downplay or try to play through sprains and dislocations, but when it comes to knee injuries, they are forced to take things seriously. The knee is the most complicated joint in the body. It is a pivotal hinge point where the bottom of the thighbone meets the top of the shinbone. Four main ligaments connect these bones. The medial collateral ligament (MCL) runs along the inner part of the knee, preventing it from bending inward. The lateral collateral ligament (LCL) runs along the outer part of the knee, preventing it from bending outward. The anterior cruciate ligament (ACL) lies in the middle of the knee and prevents the shinbone from sliding out in front of the thighbone. It stabilizes the knee. The posterior cruciate ligament (PCL) prevents the shinbone from sliding backward under the thighbone.

PCL injuries typically occur when the knee is struck from the front or hyperextended. ACL injuries are among the most common knee injuries and occur when an athlete changes direction rapidly, twists without moving the feet, lands awkwardly after jumping, or stops too suddenly. Because of the complexity of the knee joint, these injuries can become season-ending events because torn ligaments generally require surgery.

In February 2017, Kevin Durant of the Golden State Warriors sprained his MCL and had to miss many games because of his injury. This was the same injury that sidelined Stephen Curry in the first round of the 2016 playoffs. A sprained MCL can happen when a person's knee is hit or when they twist their body without moving their foot.

Knee injuries are not only serious, they are frequent, especially among female athletes, who have a rate of ACL injuries up to four times higher than males. Experts believe this may be because, compared to men, women have wider hips and looser ligaments, as well as less muscle mass and higher estrogen levels, which can make the body more prone to injury. The anatomy of the female body also causes female athletes to move differently than men, which was explained by Robert H. Shmerling, the faculty editor of Harvard Health Publications: "For example, when landing from a jump, women tend to land more upright and with the knees closer together. And when female athletes suddenly change direction, they tend to do so on one foot (perhaps due to their wider pelvis), while men tend to 'cut' from both feet."[19] This difference in motion causes more knee injuries, and female athletes are advised to practice moving in a safer way and to strengthen muscles around the knee ligaments to reduce their chances of injuring their ACL.

Basketball players can often be seen wearing knee braces to stabilize the joint after an injury.

The Dangers of Concussions

In both male and female basketball players, the head is another part of the body that is at high risk for serious injury. The most common acute injury to the head is a concussion. A concussion is typically caused when a player hits or is hit by something, most often a hard surface or another player. As a result of the blow, soft brain tissue bounces against the hard inner surface of the skull, which can cause bruising, bleeding, or tearing of nerve fibers.

Most people who sustain a concussion do not lose consciousness, but they may experience symptoms that include confusion, headache, dizziness, nausea, and sleepiness. Such symptoms commonly disappear on their own, and many athletes fail to report them if they are mild, which is dangerous because all head injuries should be examined by a knowledgeable medical professional. More severe symptoms can include convulsions, muscle weakness, vision problems, or unconsciousness, and these cannot be ignored; they often lead to an athlete being hospitalized—at least for observation.

Studies show that the risk of getting another concussion rises after a player suffers their first one, and damage from several concussions increases the risk of mental disorders, long-term memory loss, and Alzheimer's disease. Females appear to have a higher probability of suffering a concussion than males. There is no definitive answer for why this is, but experts believe that it is partly because their necks are smaller and less muscular than males' necks and thus provide less stability. Female athletes are not only more likely to be concussed, they also display more symptoms and take longer to heal:

> *[Sports physician Shannon] Bauman said concussions were often more severe in girls and women—she found differences not only in subjective reported symptoms but also in objective cognitive and visual symptoms that doctors noted during physical exams. Bauman counted objective physical signs of concussions such as trouble maintaining one's balance and vision problems, and female patients had an average of 4.5 of them, compared with 3.6 for males. "Females are reporting more symptoms, but they're also objectively having more physiological signs of concussion," Bauman said.*
>
> *The differences don't stop there. Bauman's data also showed that females take longer to heal. Thirty-four percent of men and boys who came to the clinic finished treatment within two months, yet only 12 percent of concussions in women and girls improved this fast. About 35 percent of females were still experiencing concussions six months or more after their injury.*[20]

Fast Break!

The NBA's concussion rate is the lowest among the four major U.S. sports leagues (NBA, National Football League, National Hockey League, and Major League Baseball).

Multiple Concussions and CTE

Doctors know that repeated concussions put athletes at risk for later problems, such as long-term memory loss and Alzheimer's disease. In recent years, a growing body of research has been dedicated to the study of chronic traumatic encephalopathy (CTE), which is caused by repeated brain trauma. This disease causes the brain tissue to break down over the years and for abnormal proteins to build up in the brain. In addition to memory loss and confusion, this disease can lead to problems with impulse control, aggression, depression, and suicidal tendencies.

Armed with this knowledge, medical professionals are concerned about head injuries on the court. NBA players experience very few concussions compared to players in other sports, though. There was an average of 14.9 concussions reported per NBA season from 2006 to 2014, according to a study published in 2016 in the *American Journal of Sports Medicine*. By comparison, the National Football League (NFL) reported 115 concussions in 2014. However, just because there are fewer concussions in the NBA than in other professional sports leagues, the injury is still considered serious.

Knowledgeable coaches know that players—both male and female—should not go back into a game for at least a week after a concussion to minimize further damage to the brain. In 2011, the NBA issued a new concussion protocol for players to follow. This was done to lessen chronic issues that concussions can cause and to ensure player safety. If a player is diagnosed with a concussion, he has to complete a series of tests, be evaluated by a neurologist, and be cleared to play before returning to the lineup. This process can take days to weeks, depending on the severity of the concussion.

Tough on the Tendons

Sprains, bruises, and concussions are examples of acute injuries. Blisters and shin splints (sore muscles along the shinbone in the front part of the lower legs) are examples of common chronic injuries. Chronic injuries are typically the result of overuse. They do not immediately put a player out of action, because they can take weeks or months to develop. Still, they can be extremely painful if left untreated. Early symptoms include swelling, a dull ache while a player is resting, and pain while performing activities.

Patellar tendinitis, also known as jumper's knee, is a more serious chronic injury that is caused when microscopic tears occur in the patellar tendon that connects the kneecap to the shinbone. The problem develops as a result of the repeated explosive extensions of the leg that occur when basketball players jump.

Another potentially serious chronic injury is Achilles tendinitis, which involves inflammation of the Achilles tendon—the large tendon that connects the heel to the back leg muscles. The Achilles tendon is necessary for walking and standing on tiptoe, and inflammation in it makes walking painful and sometimes impossible. This inflammation occurs when players overwork their feet.

Stress Fractures: A Result of Height?

Another common type of chronic injury is a stress fracture. Stress fractures often occur in the bones of the feet and legs of basketball players, and the damage occurs when muscles become overworked and cannot absorb the force of impact from activities such as jumping and running. The force is then placed on the bone, which develops a small crack—the stress fracture. Stress fractures can result from improper training or from overworking a body part.

Stress fractures might also be a consequence of the extreme height and weight of today's college and professional players. Although more research needs to be done on the subject, some believe that the added force of impact on the bones of taller and heavier players could cause more stress fractures, as their bodies need to absorb more force. Throughout his career, Yao Ming of the Houston Rockets, who is 7 feet 6 inches (2.3 m) tall, was sidelined with fractures in his feet. "Because of his size … and what he does playing basketball at his

Stress fractures played a large part in Yao Ming's decision to end his NBA career.

size, he is always at risk of something like this happening,"[21] said team physician Tom Clanton in 2009. In fact, when Yao Ming retired in 2011, he cited these stress fractures as factors in his decision.

Despite Yao's difficulties, stress fractures occur less frequently in males, who generally have denser bones than women. Young people of both sexes, whose bones have not reached peak density, are also at greater risk. There are no quick fixes for stress fractures. Once they occur, the best treatment is to avoid putting weight on the injury until it heals. This can obviously sideline a player for quite some time.

Diagnosing a Sports Injury

When sports injuries occur, it is important that they be properly identified and diagnosed. Doctors use several procedures to see what has happened inside the body. The most standard procedure involves X-rays, which are similar to light waves but have shorter wavelengths and can penetrate solids. X-ray machines are the first line of diagnosis for fractures. When the X-rays meet bone, the bone creates a white shadow on film because it absorbs the radiation. Where there are breaks or fractures, the X-rays pass through and show up as darker lines.

Another standard diagnostic procedure is the computerized tomography scan (CT scan), which was developed in the early 1970s. A CT scan involves multiple X-rays taken at different angles and at different levels of the body. CT scans provide three-dimensional images of an injury when an X-ray machine cannot.

Magnetic resonance imaging (MRI) is also used to diagnose sports injuries. Introduced in 1977, it does not use radiation, but instead relies on powerful magnets, radio waves, and a computer to collect hundreds of detailed images of both hard and soft tissue. The MRI scans the injury point by point, creating a precise, three-dimensional map of tissue types.

The P.R.I.C.E. of Healing

Once an injury is diagnosed, it must be properly treated. Treatment can include everything from a simple ice pack to invasive surgery, and new treatment options are being developed all the time, thanks to developments in medical technology. Howard J. Luks, chief of sports medicine and arthroscopy at Westchester Medical Center in New York City, has said, "Techniques are developing literally by the month in sports medicine ...They will provide ways to treat problems that were not treatable before, or only treatable through traditional surgery."[22]

When it comes to acute injuries such as bruises, sprains, and strains, doctors, coaches, and players follow the acronym P.R.I.C.E.: protection, rest, ice, compression, and elevation. Protection with a splint, brace, or bandage shields the injured area from further damage. Rest allows the damaged muscle, tendon, or ligament to heal. Ice, compression, and elevating the injury above the level of the heart limit swelling. Ice bags or cold packs also help to ease pain because of the anesthetic, or numbing, effect of the cold. Compression, or wrapping the injured area with a bandage, also provides additional stabilization.

Anti-inflammatory and pain-relieving medicines are another first line of treatment. In the case of acute injuries, athletes can immediately take

How Does an MRI Work?

MRI machines work because the human body is composed primarily of fat and water, both of which contain hydrogen atoms. In fact, the human body is approximately 10 percent hydrogen. The magnetic field created by the MRI machine forces hydrogen atoms in the body to line up in a way that is similar to how the needle on a compass moves when it is held near a magnet. When radio waves are sent toward the lined-up hydrogen atoms, they bounce back, and a computer records the signal. Different types of tissues send back different signals, and experts who are trained to read the results of the procedure are then able to diagnose problems that exist.

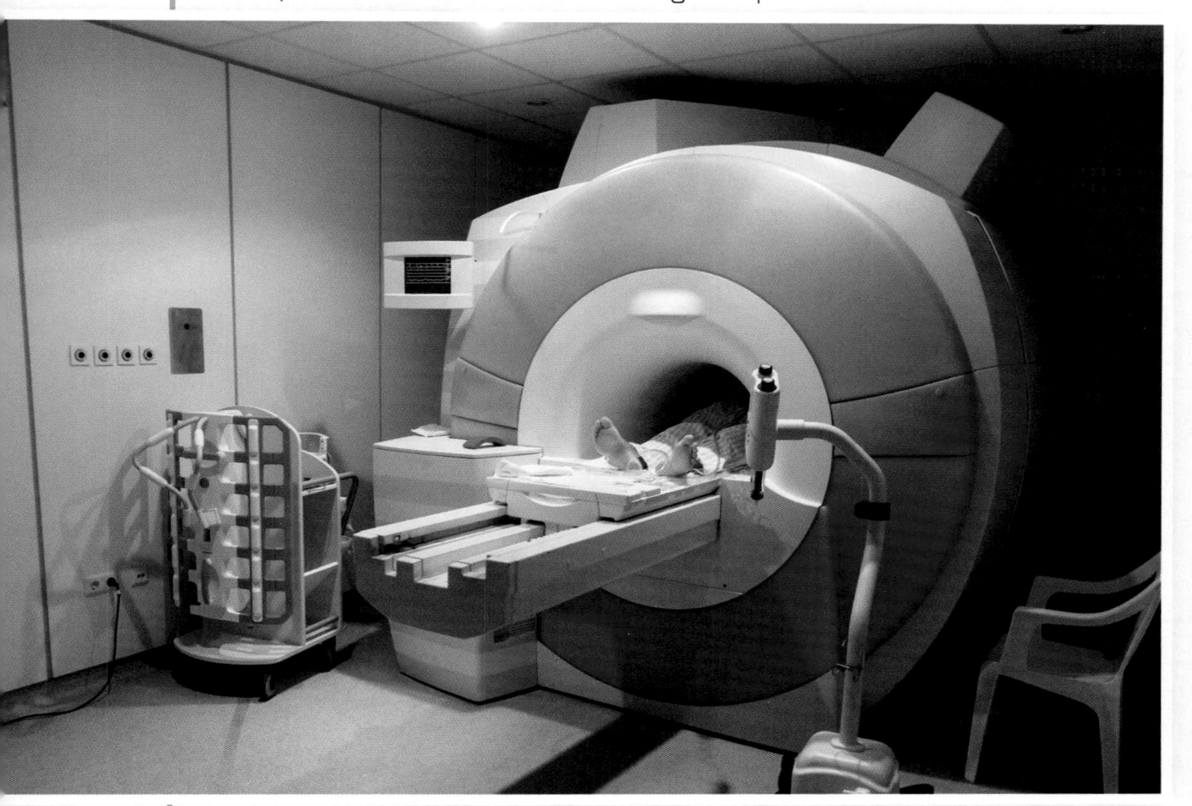

MRI machines allow doctors to diagnose injuries and help players get back on the court faster.

drugs such as aspirin, ibuprofen, and naproxen to reduce inflammation and pain. Corticosteroids—hormones such as cortisone, hydrocortisone, prednisone, and others produced by the adrenal glands or synthetically made—are also used to treat chronic soft-tissue injuries. Corticosteroids are commonly injected at the site of pain but must be used sparingly because they suppress the immune system and cause other side effects.

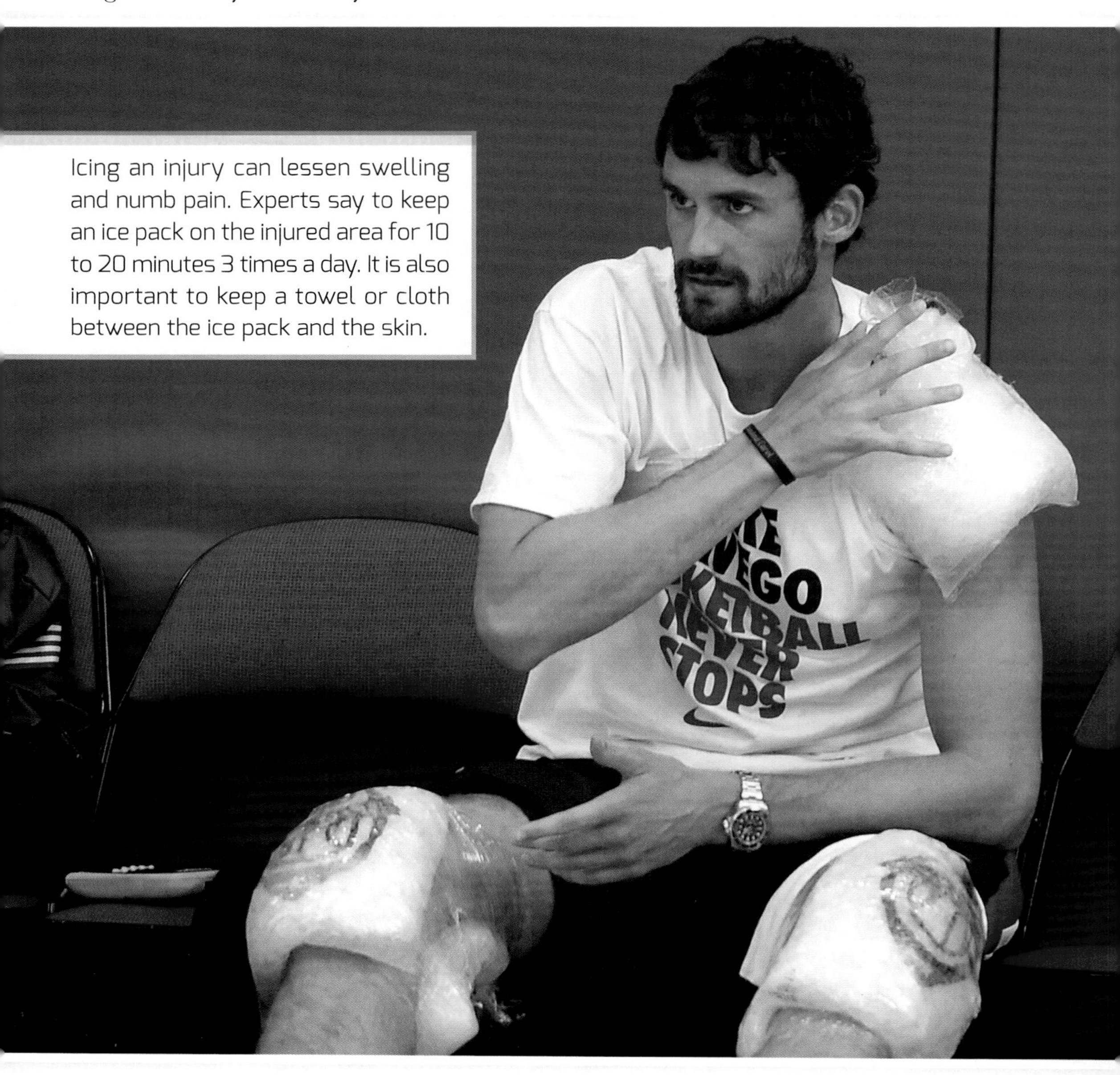

Icing an injury can lessen swelling and numb pain. Experts say to keep an ice pack on the injured area for 10 to 20 minutes 3 times a day. It is also important to keep a towel or cloth between the ice pack and the skin.

Surgical Solutions

Sometimes an injury does not respond to these basic treatments. It may be so serious that it must be surgically repaired. Torn cartilage and fractures are just two basketball injuries that often need surgery before they can heal completely.

Surgery has always been a last resort in sports, because players can miss an entire season while recovering. The latest techniques, however, speed up surgery and recovery time. One such technique is arthroscopic surgery, which is used to repair joints, especially knees. Doctors often do this kind of surgery on an outpatient basis, which means the player does not have to spend time in a hospital. No general anesthetic is used. The stress and disruption that comes with traditional surgery is reduced dramatically. According to the American Academy of Orthopaedic Surgeons, "Athletes and others who are in good physical condition may in some cases return to athletic activities within a few weeks."[23]

Arthroscopic surgery involves the use of a long, thin tube equipped with a light and a camera. The surgeon makes tiny incisions in the patient's skin, inserts the tube, and sees images of the injury on a computer screen. Pencil-sized instruments, inserted through the incisions, are used to repair the damage. Patients often are allowed to go home a few hours after the procedure.

Regaining Speed and Agility

Once basketball players recover enough, they can start rebuilding and strengthening the body part that was injured, as well as working on their overall level of fitness, which might have deteriorated if they had to be inactive for a long period of time. They must also work to regain the speed and agility they once possessed. All that improvement requires physical therapy. Physical therapists use water, massage, stretching, and gentle exercise to improve the functioning of damaged muscles, bones, and joints. NBA and WNBA teams have their own team physical therapists who work with players to rehabilitate their injuries to get them back on the court.

Light weight lifting is often uncomfortable as players strengthen or rebuild injured muscles through the use of machines or free weights. Water therapy, also known as aquatic therapy, is more comfortable. It involves slow exercises in water, using resistance to build muscle and increase the range of joint motion.

Game Changers

Serious acute injuries can end a player's career, and chronic injuries, even if they are not severe, cause many retirements, too. Injuries can force even very young players to walk away from the game. Ray Smith, a former star at the University of Arizona, officially walked away from the sport in 2016 when he was only 19 years old. Smith suffered his third ACL injury in less than three years, and the toll of those injuries proved to be too much. After Smith made his announcement, his coach, Sean Miller, explained how draining the rehabilitation process was for Smith and those who had to watch him go through it:

> *In the 25 years I have been a college basketball coach, I have never felt as helpless as I did when I saw him go down … No 19-year-old kid should have to experience three season-ending injuries in a 30-month period of time. I have watched Ray work with our strength and conditioning coach tirelessly for two years. I have seen him in our training room around the clock, doing everything he can to play the game he loves. To witness his extraordinary efforts and see this happen to him once again is beyond disheartening.*[24]

The combined effect of many injuries can also leave players with scar tissue, arthritis, and chronic pain that make an impact on their game and make it difficult for them to continue to play the sport they love. The threat of injury is always present when basketball players step on the court, but advances in equipment over the years have helped athletes avoid some of the bruises and broken bones they once suffered while playing. From courts to clothing, the development of new materials and processes has made the game safer and has allowed players to display more skill than ever before.

Chapter 4

Gear for the Game

Advanced scientific knowledge has affected every part of the sport of basketball—from how players train to how injuries are treated. It has also affected how the equipment used to play the sport has changed over time. The first basketballs were not regulated in terms of their size or inflation the way they are now. In fact, balls frequently had irregular seams, were overinflated or underinflated, and were used until they were falling apart, which made play sloppier. Even the shoes and clothing worn to play basketball have gone through major changes since the late 1800s. The shoes worn back then were made of either leather or canvas with rubber soles, and clothing was lumpy, made of wool or cotton, and could be quite uncomfortable.

Fast-forward to modern basketball, where research has provided new, synthetic (man-made) materials for clothing to keep athletes more comfortable and to improve their performance. Shoes are now custom made, jerseys wick away sweat, and equipment must be tested to meet regulations and standards. Although the equipment used to play basketball has improved greatly from its earliest days, experts continue to apply scientific knowledge to testing everything from shoes to scoreboards to see what can be made even better.

Courts and Flooring

Basketball courts have evolved from simple surfaces to high-tech systems over the years. Early courts were a simple layer of wooden planks because wood was plentiful and durable. As time passed, maple became the wood of choice. Maple is harder than other woods and thus resists scratching, splintering, and other damage. Recently, synthetic flooring made of interlocking tiles has become a popular alternative to hardwood. Synthetic flooring is designed to be more shock absorbing and thus easier on players' joints than hardwood.

Whether wood or synthetic, today's courts are more than just a single layer of flooring. A complex subfloor system lies beneath the surface material and provides additional cushioning for softer landings when players run or jump. There are many types of subfloors. Some are wood, cushioned with high-density foam. Others contain squishy rubber pads. Their job is to absorb some of the force of the impact when a player's feet touch the court. This puts less pressure on players' bodies and could help reduce joint injuries or stress fractures.

The Boston Celtics are the only NBA team to play on a floor made of a wood other than maple. The floor they play on, shown here, is made of oak.

Maple and other wood can only be used to make indoor courts, however. They can be ruined when exposed to rain, snow, or direct sunlight. For outdoor courts, such as those seen in parks and playgrounds, concrete or asphalt, which is also called blacktop, is used instead. These materials, like maple wood, are hard and provide a good surface for the ball to bounce in a predictable way. They are also able to withstand harsh weather, so aspiring NBA and WNBA stars can play outside on these courts with their friends.

A Better Bounce

Hardwood, concrete, and asphalt are the ideal surfaces for a basketball court because they are hard materials. They absorb less energy than soft materials, such as carpeting. When a basketball bounces, some of its energy is absorbed by whatever surface it touches. The smaller the amount of energy absorbed by the surface, the more energy remains in the ball for it to bounce back. This is why a ball bounced on a rug will not bounce as high as one bounced on wood or concrete.

Measuring Up

All NBA courts are made of the same basic material, and they are also the same size and shape. A regulation NBA court is a rectangle with two sides that are 94 feet (28.65 m) long and two sides that are 50 feet (15.24 m) long. This means the area of a regulation NBA court, which is found by multiplying the length of the court by the width, is 4,700 square feet (436.63 sq m).

Within that rectangle are other lines and shapes, with one of the most important being the three-point line. This line, which is found on both ends of the court, curves to form a semicircle, with the basket at its center. The distance from a spot on most of the three-point line to the basket on an NBA court is 23.75 feet (7.24 m). This is called the arc radius. Arc radius measures the distance from the center of a circle to a point on an arc, or part, of that circle. NBA players get an extra point—three instead of two—for making a shot at this distance or beyond it. Although the arc radius stays the same around most of the three-point line, a basketball court is not wide enough for the line to form a perfect semicircle. It actually becomes a straight line as it nears the edge of the court, which is also known as the baseline. This part of the three-point line is only 22 feet (6.71 m) from the basket. However, players can easily get pushed out of bounds there, so the shot is still worth an extra point.

The arc radius of the three-point line differs for different levels and leagues. For example, the three-point line for both FIBA and the WNBA has an arc radius of 22.15 feet (6.75 m) for most of the semicircle and a distance of 21.65 feet (6.6 m) at the baseline. The court used for men's NCAA games has a three-point line that is 20.75 feet (6.32 m) from the basket. The difference between college courts and professional courts means that players have a small adjustment to make when they reach the highest level of the sport, and taking math into account helps them make that adjustment.

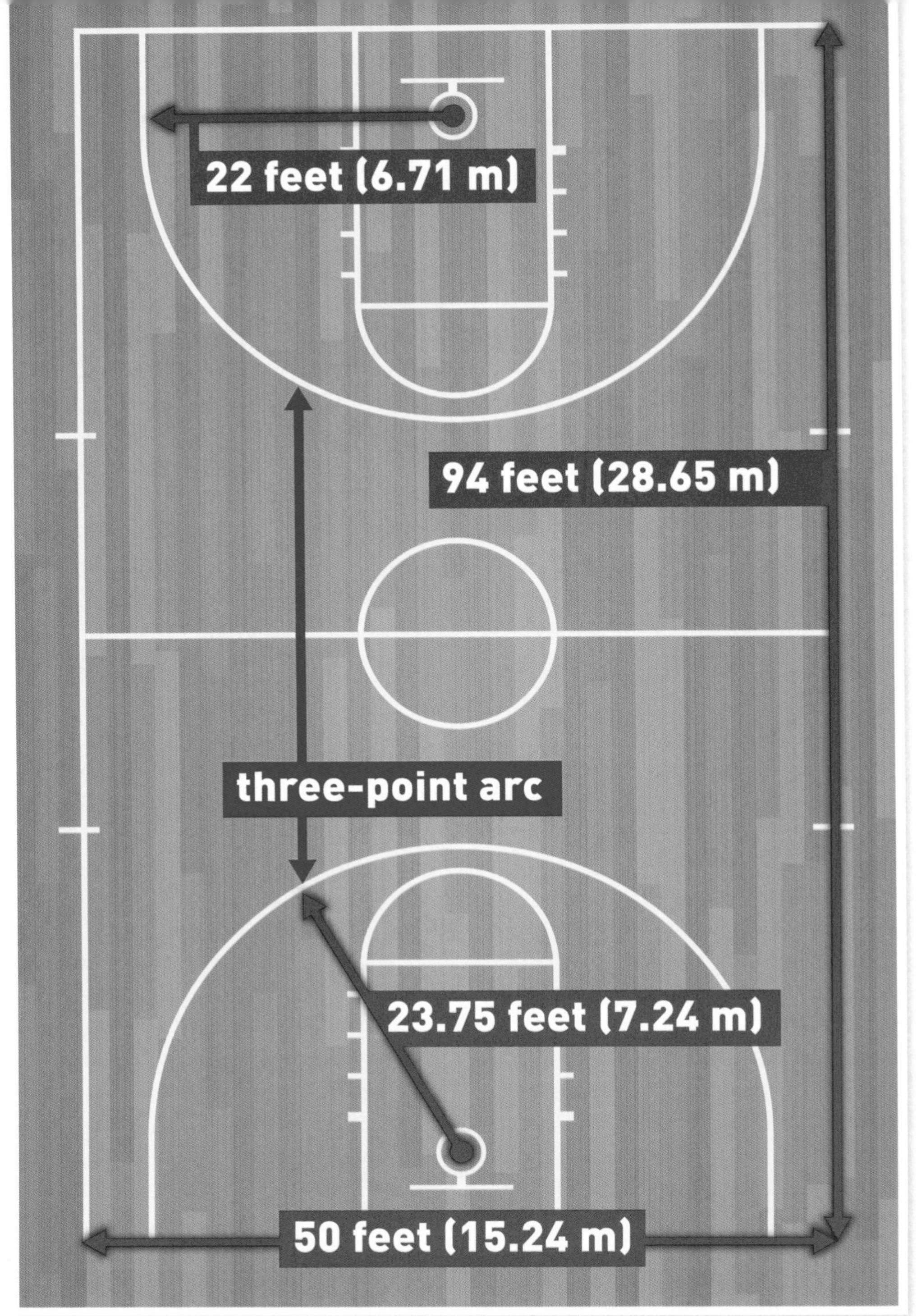

Shown here are the dimensions of a regulation NBA court. All courts in this league must have the same dimensions to ensure fair play.

Ball Basics

Basketball was originally played with a soccer ball. The first official basketball was manufactured by the sporting goods company Spalding in 1894. It was made of laced leather with a rubber bladder inside that was inflated to help the ball keep its shape. Laces remained a part of Spalding basketballs until 1937.

Today, nearly all basketballs are made of an inflatable inner rubber bladder covered with either leather, rubber, or a synthetic composite, which is a mixture of materials. Official NBA basketballs are made of leather, while basketballs made of rubber are commonly used on outdoor courts. Rubber is more durable than leather, so it is used on rougher court surfaces, such as concrete. In 2006, the NBA began using composite basketballs that are made to feel like leather. These balls are cheaper than leather balls, and their surface does not wear down as easily. However, the players preferred the leather ball, so composite basketballs are no longer used in the NBA.

No matter what a ball is made of, it will not bounce unless it is properly inflated. Variations in inflation affect the way the ball bounces. A basketball that is correctly inflated will bounce higher with less effort than a basketball of the same size that is underinflated. This is because air inside the ball is made up of particles called molecules that have weight and volume and are in constant motion. The more molecules of air that are inside the ball, the more crowded they are and the more they move and push on the inner surface of the ball. This creates air pressure and makes the ball firm. A ball with too little air is soft and difficult to bounce. With too much air pressure, however, the ball rebounds too high and is less controllable.

The recommended inflation pressure for basketballs is between 7 and 9 pounds per square inch (psi). The organizations that use the balls dictate the precise pressure range. NBA balls must be inflated to between 7.5 and 8.5 psi. The WNBA has similar requirements. It is important for the balls to be inflated to a psi precisely within this range because even a small change in psi can affect how a ball bounces on the court, which can impact the whole game.

The first basketballs looked very different from the basketballs used today.

From Period-Appropriate to Practical

Of all basketball equipment, uniforms have changed most visibly over the years. Early uniforms were quite different from the functional, comfortable sports gear worn today. Then, male basketball players wore long pants or pants that were cut just below the knee. Female basketball players wore long skirts and long-sleeved, high neck blouses. These uniforms might have been appropriate for the time period, but they were not good for athletic activity. The bulky clothing made it difficult for players to move because it weighed them down and restricted their range of motion. The long skirts the women wore were also unsafe; it was easy to trip and fall when playing basketball in a floor-length skirt.

As years passed, uniforms became more practical. Men adopted sleeveless wool jerseys and cotton shorts, which allowed them to move easily. Women gave up their skirts and put on knee-length bloomers. A few daring women's teams began dressing in shorts and short-sleeved shirts, which kept players cooler and allowed greater freedom of movement.

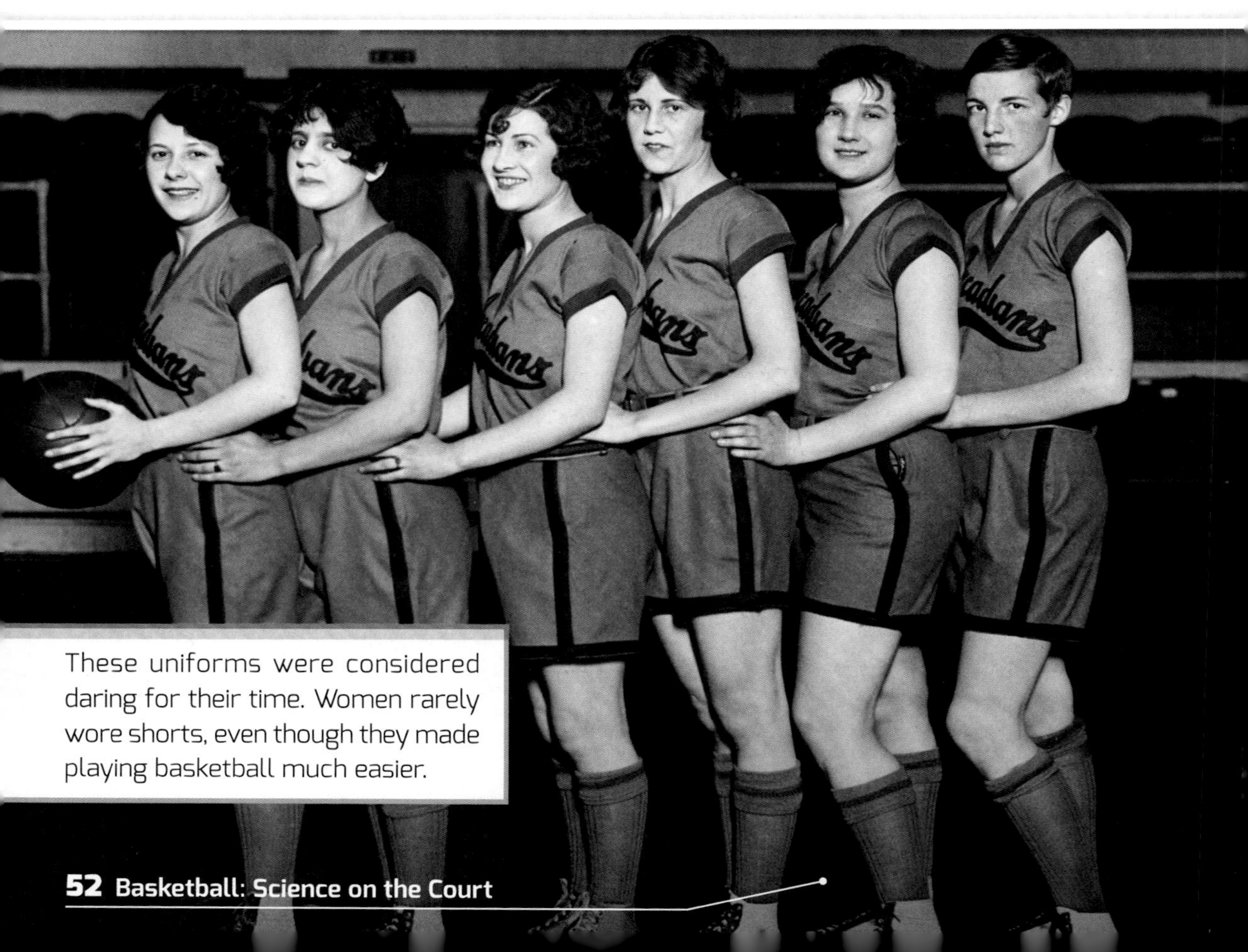

These uniforms were considered daring for their time. Women rarely wore shorts, even though they made playing basketball much easier.

Sleeves: Protection or Personal Style?

On today's basketball courts, it is common to see players wearing sleeves on their arms or legs. These compression sleeves have many purposes, but one of the chief reasons players wear them is to improve circulation. Compression sleeves compress, or squeeze, the blood vessels in the body part they cover. This causes increased blood flow to muscles, which could help reduce soreness and improve muscle performance in athletes. Some basketball players, such as Allen Iverson, wear compression sleeves while recovering from an injury, because the increased blood flow they cause can promote healing and the sleeve can act as another layer of protection for the injured body part.

There are both scientific and stylistic reasons for these sleeves. Although some basketball players use compression sleeves for medical reasons, others have been known to wear them because they like the way they look. They can also be used to hide tattoos.

A sleeve can help a basketball player keep their shooting arm warm. This keeps the muscles loose and could boost the player's performance on the court.

Today, every article of clothing used in team play is designed for comfort and practicality. Fabrics are made of synthetic materials, such as polyester or microfiber knits or meshes, which are stretchy and comfortable. Microfiber material is known for its softness, durability, and moisture-wicking abilities. Moisture-wicking fabrics are made with tiny holes that pull sweat away from the skin to keep players dry. They also allow for air circulation to keep players cooler. Recently developed antimicrobial fabrics hinder the growth of bacteria to control odors and keep uniforms smelling fresher.

Fast Break!

Basketball players who do not wear a mouth guard are six times more likely to suffer a serious dental injury or concussion than players who do wear a mouth guard.

Footwear: At the Sole of Basketball

Shoes are an important part of a basketball player's uniform. Because basketball players run on a floor that is made of wood, which can be slippery, their shoes need to create just the right amount of friction—a force that exists when something moves across a surface to slow its motion. If the shoes do not create enough friction, players can slip and fall, possibly injuring themselves. However, if the shoes create too much friction, the player will not be able to run quickly or change directions easily.

In the early days of the sport, basketball players wore whatever shoes they found comfortable enough to play in. Things began to change in 1908, when shoe manufacturer Marquis Mills Converse founded the Converse Rubber Shoe Company in Chicago, Illinois. Basketball players recognized the benefits of rubber soles that gripped the court, which helped create more friction than previous basketball shoes, and began wearing them during games.

In 1917, Converse introduced the first basketball shoe. The Converse All Star was a simple, canvas high top with a rubber sole. When former basketball player Charles H. "Chuck" Taylor became a spokesman for the company in 1921, his salesmanship pushed them into the public eye. A pair of Converse All Stars, nicknamed "Chucks," became a must-have item for basketball players as well as young people across the country. Basketball players almost exclusively wore Converse shoes until the 1970s, which was when companies such as Adidas and Nike began promoting their own lines of basketball shoes.

Basketball shoe construction and performance on the court must meet the demands of the professional game. The game puts great stress and strain on basketball players' feet, so they need something that is supportive, flexible, shock absorbing, and able to provide

Converse All Stars were the first shoes made specifically for basketball players. These shoes are still popular today, but they are no longer worn by professional basketball players because other shoes provide better support.

proper traction or grip. To achieve all these things, manufacturers focus on four parts of the shoe: the upper, insole, midsole, and outsole.

The uppers of basketball shoes are the portions above the soles. They provide support around the foot and ankle to keep the ankle from rolling over and to reduce pressure on the Achilles tendon, but they are still soft enough to allow flexibility. They are padded, vented, and lined with moisture-wicking fabric so the foot can remain as cool and dry as possible.

Insoles are found under the sole of the foot. They are firm to support players' arches. Many players replace insoles with custom-made inserts often called orthotics, which are designed to relieve pressure on certain areas of the foot or to correct positioning of the lower body. Improper positioning can stem from such irregularities as overpronation (rolling in of the foot) or leg length discrepancy (one leg being shorter than the other). Without proper alignment, players can suffer ankle, knee, hip, and lower back pain.

Sandwiched between the insole and the bottom of the shoe (called the outsole), is the midsole, which has been the focus of shoe research for more than a quarter of a century. The midsole provides cushioning and protection for the foot, and it absorbs shocks to protect the knees and ankles. It must be light enough so the shoe is not too heavy, slightly spongy to absorb the force of impact with the court, and extremely durable. Manufacturers are constantly creating new materials and shock-absorbing systems for the midsoles of basketball shoes to improve player performance.

Fast Break!

Shaquille O'Neal wore a size 22 basketball shoe, which was the biggest ever at the time he played in the NBA.

The Science of Soles

Most basketball midsoles are made of either polyurethane or ethylene vinyl acetate (EVA) foams or pellets (known as Phylon). Polyurethane is stiffer and heavier than EVA but lasts longer. EVA is softer and more flexible, but it becomes flattened over time as the air is squeezed out. Once EVA is compressed, it no longer provides cushioning. Therefore, midsoles are often made of a combination of materials and often contain cushions filled with air or gel to help shock absorption. As journalist Tim Newcomb stated, "Cushioning isn't a one-type fit for all."[25]

Outsoles are the parts of the shoe that come in contact with the ground. They are typically made of real or synthetic rubber. Some are made of lightweight blown synthetic rubber, which contain air pockets to provide extra cushioning. Rubber is the material of choice for outsoles because it helps players' feet grip the court in a forward direction but slide easily while shuffling or pivoting sideways.

Although players are always looking for gear that gives them an edge over their opponents, they must also pay attention to the scientific principles that affect how their gear performs and that control their every move on the court. Physics, which is the science of matter and energy, plays a part in every aspect of a basketball game, and understanding physics helps basketball players better understand everything about the sport they play—from which shoes to wear to how to execute a successful slam dunk.

Charged Cushioning

Basketball players move in a variety of ways during a game, so it is helpful for them to wear a shoe that provides cushioning and support for specific movements. This was what Under Armour had in mind when it developed its Charged Cushioning midsole. According to *Sports Illustrated* writer Tim Newcomb,

> *Developed in a partnership with Dow Chemical, the [Charged Cushioning] foam feels soft under low loads such as jumping up and down for a jump shot, but becomes firmer under high loads, such as exploding for a quick first step. The responsiveness reduces impact and provides a high-energy return for the player.*[1]

The Charged Cushioning foam changes in response to changes in a player's movements, which is beneficial for players who are known for their speed and offensive skills. This is why the foam was chosen as the featured midsole material in Under Armour's Curry One shoe, which was designed for Stephen Curry, who is known as one of the NBA's best offensive players.

1. Tim Newcomb, "Stepping Softly: Getting to the Bottom of Basketball Sneaker Cushioning," *Sports Illustrated*, April 3, 2015. www.si.com/nba/2015/04/03/investigating-sneaker-cushioning-nike-adidas-jordan.

Chapter 5

Physics and Basketball

Training, injury treatment, and equipment are all examples of the ways science is applied to basketball. Science explains why certain training methods work, why injuries happen, and why equipment is made the way it is. Basketball is a game that relies heavily on physics, which is the science of matter and energy and how they interact. Every bounce of the ball, pass to a teammate, and slam dunk can be explained through the study of how the physical world behaves.

Through physics, we learn why objects act the way they do, why they move, why they change direction, and why they stop. This knowledge is incredibly helpful when taking a closer look at the sport of basketball. As *Wired* magazine writer Aatish Bhatia stated, "In a way, a game like basketball is a physics geek's delight. It's a playground where you can apply physics principles to try and get some added insight to the game. You've got the interplay of projectile motion and collisions, energy and momentum, and so on."[26] Physics helps basketball fans make sense of the amazing feats they see on the court, and relating physics concepts to an exciting sport such as basketball helps people find the fun in science.

Doing Work

"Energy" is an important word in both physics and basketball. Energy is commonly associated with vigorous activity, as in "The players are running and jumping. They have lots of energy." In physics, however, energy has a more scientific definition: the ability of a physical system to do work. Everything—from human beings to basketballs—has energy, and the law of conservation of energy states that energy can be transferred, but it cannot be destroyed. Science and technology educator David Watson explained the law of conservation of energy in this way: "Energy can be stored. Energy can move from one bunch or piece of matter to another bunch or piece of matter. Energy can be transformed from one type of energy to another type of energy. [But] during all this moving and transforming the total amount of energy never changes."[27]

A basketball game is an event that allows people to see many physics concepts in action.

In basketball, as in everything else, two kinds of energy are always at play—kinetic and potential. Kinetic energy is energy of motion. The more an object weighs and the faster it is moving, the more kinetic energy it has. A ball flying through the air has kinetic energy, and so does a player jumping. Kinetic energy can transform into potential energy, which is stored energy. This can happen when a basketball player catches the ball, stopping its motion. Potential energy exists as an object's potential for movement or for doing work. For example, a ball held in the air by a player has potential energy because when it is released, it will fall. When this happens, the potential energy is transformed into kinetic energy because the ball is moving. When an object is in motion, it changes its position. The rate at which it does this is its velocity. A change in velocity is known as acceleration. Velocity and acceleration are both important concepts in basketball because the ball and the players change positions so often.

Sir Isaac Newton's Laws

Seventeenth-century mathematician and physicist Sir Isaac Newton was one of the most important scientists of all time. He first published his laws of motion in the 1680s and used them to explain and investigate the movement of many physical objects and systems. Without his contributions, the development of modern technology would have been impossible.

Netwon's first law: If an object is at rest, it will remain at rest unless an outside force acts on it. If an object is moving, it will continue to move in a straight line at the same speed until an outside force acts on it. This is also known as the law of inertia, because inertia is the property of an object to resist a change in its motion.

Newton's second law: When a force acts on an object, the object will accelerate in relation to the force and the mass of the object. If the mass of an object stays constant, increasing force will increase acceleration. If the force on an object remains constant, increasing the object's mass will decrease acceleration.

Newton's third law: For every action there is an equal and opposite reaction; the forces of two bodies on each other are always equal and directed in opposite directions.

He Shoots, He ... Transfers Energy!

Shooting the ball toward the hoop involves several kinds of energy. For instance, the ball in the player's hands has potential energy. The player transfers energy to the ball by pushing it into the air with their hands. The ball flying through the air then has kinetic energy.

The push that sends the ball flying toward the hoop is called a force. A force is anything that causes change in the motion or shape of an object. A push or a pull is a force. Any force applied to an object is fittingly known as applied force. When force is applied to push the ball, the ball accelerates in the direction of the force according to how much force is applied, which is also known as its magnitude. This is the basis of Isaac Newton's second law of motion.

Newton noted that force has both magnitude—the power of the push or pull—and direction. If the mass—the amount of matter in an object—remains the same, more force results in greater acceleration and less force means less acceleration. Newton determined that the magnitude of a force can be calculated by multiplying the mass of the object being pushed or pulled by the acceleration of the object.

Isaac Newton, shown here, changed the way people looked at the physical world and the motion of objects when he introduced his three laws of motion.

Fast Break!

In Oak Park, California, in 2014, Elan Buller made the longest basketball shot to date. It traveled for 112.5 feet (34.3 m).

Projectile Motion

When the basketball accelerates through the air toward the basket, it becomes a projectile. A projectile is an object that, once put in motion by a force, continues in motion by its own inertia and is influenced only by the downward force of gravity. Inertia is the tendency of objects to resist change in motion. Newton explained inertia in his first law of motion. He said that, without a force to start it, an object will never begin moving. However, once an object is moving, it will never stop unless acted upon by a force.

Gravity is one force that changes the motion of the ball. Gravity is the force of attraction between two objects. The larger the masses, the bigger the pull of gravity, so on Earth, the strongest pull of gravity is toward the planet's center. A basketball shot into the air will continue upward until its acceleration lessens and becomes unable to overcome the pull of gravity. Then, the object starts to come down. The upside-down U-shaped path that the ball takes as it goes up and then comes down is called its parabolic path. A parabola is a curved shape that resembles a U. Another word for a parabolic path is projectile motion.

An Underhanded Attempt

In 2016, a rookie NBA player brought back what is known as the "granny shot," an underhand way of shooting a foul shot. In fact, Houston Rockets rookie Chinanu Onuaku is the first NBA player since Rick Barry in the 1970s to use this method. However, according to physics, the odds of scoring are much better when using this underhand technique. As Curtis Rist explained in *Discover* magazine,

> *The key to a successful foul shot lies in the arc of the ball—in general, the higher the better. While an official-size basket is 18 inches [45.7 cm] in diameter, the basketball itself is only about 9 1/2 inches [24.1 cm], which gives a margin of 8 1/2 inches [21.6 cm]. But when the ball is thrown nearly straight at the basket ... the margin disappears because the rim of the basket, from the perspective of the ball, resembles a tight ellipse [an oval shape]. "That's why these*

1. Curtis Rist, "Physics Proves It: Everyone Should Shoot Granny-Style," *Discover*, August 7, 2008. discovermagazine.com/2008/the-body/07-physics-proves-it-everyone-should-shoot-granny-style.

guys miss so much," [physicist Peter] Brancazio says. "Because of the sharp angle of the typical overhand throw, there ends up being a much smaller window for the ball to go in." If the ball comes down at the basket from a steeper angle, the way it does if tossed up in the high arc characteristic of an underhand throw, the margin reappears. "That means there's a far greater chance of making the basket," he says.[1]

Chinanu Onuaku has become famous for his "granny shot" technique.

For players to get the ball where they want it to go when they shoot, they have to take into account inertia, gravity, and where their target is in relation to where they are standing. The last factor is very important. The basket may be almost directly overhead or far across the court. Thus, players must push the ball into the air at the correct angle and with the correct amount of force if they want to get the ball through the hoop.

The movement of the basketball in the air is also known as its trajectory.

Angling for Success

An angle is defined as the space between two intersecting lines. The line can be real or imaginary. In practical terms, an angle looks like a slice of pie. The inner point of the slice (where the lines intersect, or meet) is called the vertex, and its sides are the lines, which can also be called rays. Angles are measured in degrees and can range in size from 0 degrees to 360 degrees. A 360-degree angle looks like a whole pie—a circle. A 90-degree angle looks like a quarter of a pie—an L shape. A 0-degree angle looks like no pie at all; it appears as a straight line.

The angle at which players release a ball when shooting is called the release angle or launch angle. The vertex is at their hands, and the rays are imaginary lines—one that runs parallel to the floor and one that follows the path of the ball when it leaves their hands. Experts have determined that players can always send the ball to the center of the hoop if they create the correct release angle. That angle would depend on the height of the ball from the court, the shooter's distance from the hoop, and the force used to propel the ball. By knowing those variables, the angle can be computed:

> *We know from theory and experiment that you get the most distance with the least effort by firing a projectile at 45 degrees, exactly midway between vertical and horizontal. And we can assume that least-effort shooting is really important for a player taking a jump shot, because he or she can't push against the floor for power, especially in heavy defensive traffic. So the fastest and easiest angle would seem to be 45 degrees.*
>
> *Except when it isn't, which is a lot of the time. The reason is that 45 degrees is the ideal least-effort angle* only *if the ball is shot from the same height as the basket, which is 10 feet [3 m] above the floor. So it's perfect for a 7-foot [2.1 m] player whose arms reach 2 feet [0.6 m] over his or her head and who jumps 1 foot [0.3 m] off the floor to shoot. The rest of us will be launching the ball "uphill" … So we'll need larger angles …*
>
> *[Physics expert Peter] Brancazio explains that you need 45 degrees plus half the angle formed by a straight line between the position of the ball at launch and the basket. Depending on your height and where you are on the court, that typically ranges from 7 to 14 degrees. Thus, for a shot leaving your hands at 8 feet [2.4 m] above the floor from 18 feet [5.5 m] out, you'll want to launch the ball at a bit more than 48 degrees. For most players at a distance of 10 to 25 feet [3 to 7.6 m], the least-effort angle ranges between 47 and 52 degrees.*
>
> *Using that system, you can calculate the ideal free-throw angle. It's 13.75 feet [4.2 m] from the free-throw line to the center of the basket, and a 6-foot [1.8 m] player launches the ball from*

Basketball players practice the positioning of their hands when they shoot the ball to create the best launch angle for successful shots.

about 7 feet [2.1 m] above the hardwood. That works out to a shooting angle of 51 degrees.

Of course, Brancazio did his calculations long before the advent of the modern computer. But a new state-of-the-art study gives basically the same result. Last November, engineers at North Carolina State University published an analysis of hundreds of thousands of 3-D computer simulations of free throws. Their optimal angle: 52 degrees.[28]

Obviously, the accuracy required to calculate and carry out such shots during the course of a game is impossible. That is why no basketball player is able to make a basket every time they shoot. However, the best shooters know that if they are consistent about when and where they release the ball and release it with a smooth motion to get consistent speed, they will hit the basket more often. Larry Silverberg, a mechanical and aerospace engineer, studied hundreds of thousands of three-dimensional computer simulations of basketball free-throw trajectories and confirmed that fact. He has stated, "A little bit of physics and a lot of practice can make everyone a better shooter."[29]

Physics Leads to Points

If players have the knowledge and control to use the correct force and angles when shooting a basket, the ball ends up at the hoop. If a ball drops squarely into the basket, gravity pulls it down, and points are scored. If the ball hits the rim of the hoop or the backboard, other forces come into play.

When a ball hits the backboard or the rim of the basket, it encounters a force that sends it bouncing away, according to Newton's third law of motion. It does not bounce away with the same amount of force, however, because the rim or backboard absorbs a small amount of energy, and a small amount is lost due to friction—the force that resists movement between two objects. The rougher the objects, the more friction there is between them. When the ball hits or rubs against the rim, it slows. If it hits the upper part of the rim, that slowing gives it a better chance of dropping into the basket. Physics professor and basketball expert John J. Fontanella has written, "Good shooters minimize the speed of the basketball at the rim. The effect of friction is to decrease the speed further. This helps any shooter."[30]

The angle at which the ball bounces away is called the rebound angle, and it is the same as the angle of entry, the angle at which the ball approached the backboard or the rim. If the ball hits the outer rim as it is coming toward the basket, it will rebound or bounce back away from the rim at that same angle. Players learn that hitting the outer front part of the rim, known as "shooting short," will never lead to points, because the ball will always bounce away from the basket. If they hit the backboard or the back of the rim from the top, though, they have a good chance of sending the ball into the basket if its rebound angle is correct.

The Benefits of Backspin

A basketball is more likely to bounce off a backboard and angle down through the hoop if the player gives it backspin. Backspin is rotation on a ball that reverses its forward motion. Bhatia stated, "You can see that it isn't luck, but physics, that makes shots with backspin likelier to land in the hoop."[31] With backspin, the ball rotates backward at the same time it flies through the air. Because it is spinning backward when it hits the backboard, it slows down more upon hitting the rim because more friction exists between the ball and the surface it hits due to the additional movement of the ball. It also has more of a tendency to bounce in the direction of its spin, which is downward and backward, toward the net. "Backspin deadens the ball [reduces its upward energy] when it bounces off the rim or backboard … giving [it] a better chance of settling through the net,"[32] writer Mick Kulikowski stated in an analysis on the physics of free throws.

Players produce backspin by flicking their wrists forward and down as the ball rolls off their fingers when they shoot. This motion starts the ball spinning toward them. Although the ball is spinning backward, the greater force of their arms pushes it forward through the air. When backspin is correctly combined with the right trajectory, proper amount of friction, force of gravity, and launch angle, the ball takes a path down through the hoop. If the combination of forces is wrong, the shot is missed.

It has been calculated that shooters should launch their shots with about 3 hertz of backspin. A hertz is a unit of frequency equal to 1 cycle per second. That means the ball should make three complete backspinning revolutions before reaching the hoop to achieve the best results. Because most players do not have the time or control needed to determine the frequency of their backspin in a game, practice is again the best way to create a consistent shooting motion without having to think about the science behind it during a game.

Going Vertical

Players need to be able to handle the ball well to get it into the basket, and at the same time, they need good jumping skills. Slam dunks and layups are plays that require players to bend their knees and use their leg muscles to push off the floor with explosive force. The best jumpers get farther off the ground because they weigh less or have more powerful leg muscles than other players.

An average NBA player can jump vertically 28 inches (71.1 cm). It may seem that taller players would have the best vertical jump heights, but the height of the players is not always an indication of their vertical jump. Retired NBA star Spudd Webb is only 5 feet 7 inches (1.7 m) tall, but he had a vertical jump of 42 inches (107 cm). Webb could jump almost as high as superstar Michael Jordan, who is 6 feet 6 inches (2 m) tall and had a vertical jump of 48 inches (121.9 cm). A player with smaller mass, such as Webb, needs less force to move their body, which makes it easier on their body to execute a vertical jump.

Vertical jumps are important, but players seldom move straight upward when they jump during a game. Instead, they take a few steps and then launch themselves forward and upward in a parabolic arc similar to the path a ball follows when it is thrown. Despite the fact that their bodies travel in an arc, many appear to defy the laws of gravity and hang in the air for a time. Nobel-Prize-winning scientist Kary Mullis has stated, "It seems they are not really following a physical trajectory sometimes. Now whether that's the truth or not, it feels that way, anyway. They just keep hanging up there."[33]

What Is Hang Time?

"Hang time" is the time during which basketball players seem to float in the air when they jump. Michael Jordan was known for his hang time. However,

Michael Jordan was known during his time in the NBA for his impressive hang time. However, even the best players are brought back down to Earth by the force of gravity.

hang time is an illusion. The player is not actually suspended in the air. During a jump, the body moves up and forward, reaches a high point, and then comes down. The player is not actually defying gravity; they are simply exerting force through their body to overcome gravity's pull for a short period of time before landing back on the ground. They are still being pulled down to Earth; it just appears to be taking longer for them to come down than it takes other people.

The illusion is created through two ways of moving. First, players move their arms upward and pull their legs up as they reach the height of their leap. This heightens the impression of upward movement. Second, they actually lengthen the time they are in the air by leaping forward as well as upward. The physics of the trajectory does the rest.

At the beginning and end of the trajectory, vertical speed is greatest, while at the top of the trajectory, just before players start coming down, vertical speed nears zero. Therefore, as a basketball player nears the highest part of their jump, they are not moving vertically as much as they are moving horizontally. They are also in the air longest during this time, and they are highly visible. Coupled with techniques such as lifting the arms and legs to give the appearance of upward motion, the combination works so they appear to be defying gravity. In addition, according to Bhatia, "Basketball players appear to float because they spend 71 percent of their 'hang time' in the top half of their jump. If they're moving towards the hoop as well, then 71 percent of that horizontal distance is covered while they're in the top half of their jump, adding to the illusion of floating."[34]

Stronger Players, Stronger Baskets

As professional basketball players have developed better training techniques to grow stronger, the equipment used to play the sport has developed with them. For example, the glass backboards used in the NBA could easily shatter from being hit with the ball, but backboards are now treated with special chemicals or created using extreme heat and cold to make them stronger.

In addition, the rims of the baskets have been made stronger over the years to withstand the force of powerful slam dunks. These rims are designed to bounce back when players push on the rim during a slam dunk. This flexibility makes the rim and backboard less likely to break under the increased force.

The Complex Science of Dribbling

In addition to jumping and shooting, basketball players spend a great deal of time dribbling. In this move, energy, gravity, friction, and angles all play significant roles. The ball has potential energy when it is held in the player's hands. Its potential energy becomes kinetic energy as soon as it is pushed downward. Gravity pulls it downward, too, so coupled with the force from the player, the downward movement is faster than it would be if the ball were pulled by gravity alone.

The moment the ball hits the floor, kinetic energy again becomes potential energy, and some of it is lost through friction. As explained in an article in *Scientific American* magazine,

> *When a basketball bounces, it has two different types of energy: kinetic and potential. Kinetic is the energy an object has due to its motion. Potential energy is that which is stored in an object—its potential for motion—such as due to its height above the ground. For example, when you hold a basketball at waist level, it has some potential energy. If you drop the basketball, the force of gravity pulls it down, and as the ball falls its potential energy is converted to kinetic energy. When a basketball hits a court floor, a part of the kinetic energy gets converted into sound or heat, some of it briefly changes the ball's shape (flattening it slightly) and a portion is absorbed by the floor surface.*[35]

Because of lost energy and the force needed to overcome the pull of gravity, when the ball bounces upward, it does not rise to its original height. When the ball hits the court, the court pushes back with an equal and opposite reaction according to Newton's third law of motion. However, as the force of each bounce lessens, the upward force exerted by the court also lessens. Each bounce that follows drains energy, so eventually, the ball settles to the floor. For that reason, dribbling requires the player's hand to add energy in the form of a push after each bounce.

Just as when they shoot, players must take angles into account when they dribble. When a ball is thrown from a player's hand to the floor, it creates what is known as an angle of incidence, measured between the floor and the ball's path. If the ball travels straight down, the angle of incidence is 90 degrees. Angles of incidence are always 90 degrees or less. The angle at which the ball travels away from the floor after the bounce is called the angle of reflection. The law of reflection states that under ideal conditions, the angle of incidence always equals the angle of reflection, so the ball always bounces up and away at the same angle that it hits the floor. Ideal conditions mean that the ball is perfectly round; the floor is hard, flat, and perfectly clean; and the ball is not spinning.

Soft Hands

Passing and catching are another pair of essential basketball skills. To successfully catch a pass, a player needs to be able to absorb some of the kinetic energy from the moving ball. A ball will not bounce off a flexible surface, such as a pillow, the same way it will bounce off a hard surface, such as a brick wall. At the moment of impact, the flexible surface moves a little in the direction the ball is already going. The surface acts as a cushion, sinking in slightly to absorb some of the ball's force when the two objects collide. This will reduce the ball's tendency to bounce the opposite way. The wall, on the other hand, will not flex at the moment of collision. It will not cushion the impact or absorb the ball's energy, so the ball's movement in the opposite direction after the impact will be greater. To catch a ball, then, basketball players must try to cushion it with their hands—to absorb some of the moving ball's energy at the moment of impact. They do this by allowing their fingers, hands, arms, and even feet to move a little in the same direction the ball is already going. This way, when the ball connects with the player's hands, most of its energy is absorbed, not deflected. The ball will then remain in their hands instead of bouncing off of them. Catching the ball this way gives the ball more time to slow down and adds to the time that energy is

transferring. It also reduces some of the stinging sensation or pain that can happen when the ball hits a player's hands too hard.

A player is said to have "soft hands" when their hands absorb the impact of the ball: "Soft hands is a term that

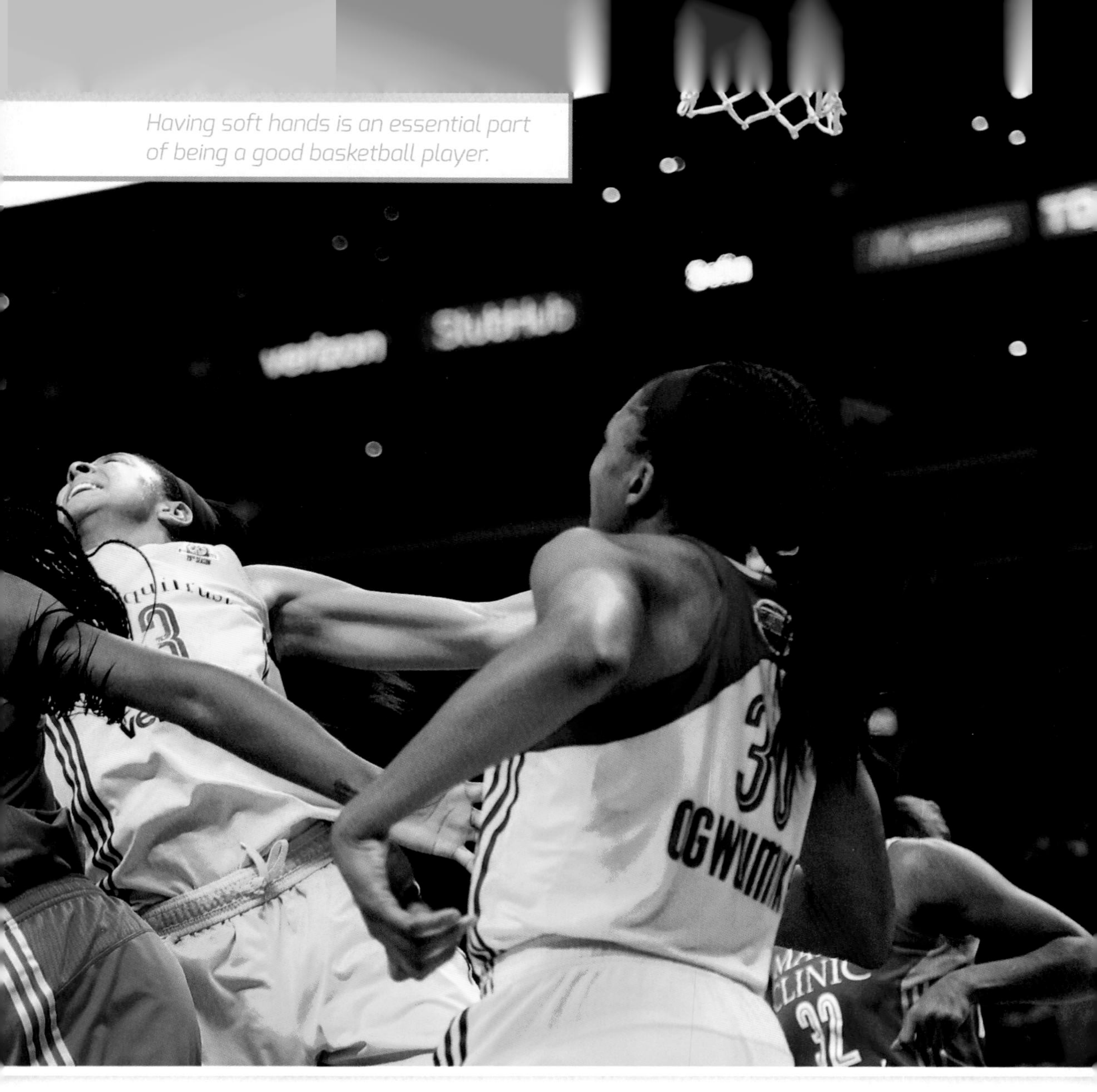

Having soft hands is an essential part of being a good basketball player.

is used to describe a players' ability to handle the basketball regardless of how hard or soft it comes at them. They seem to be able to control everything."[36]

Whether it is in developing soft hands, better balance, or any other skill needed on the court, players' knowledge of their physical abilities and how their body works is another important part of basketball. Shooting, dunking, dribbling, and passing are examples of physics, but they are also examples of another branch of science—biomechanics—in action.

Chapter 6

The Biomechanics of Basketball

Basketball players often act like machines on the court, so it is helpful to study their movements through the lens of biomechanics—the study of the mechanics of the human body, especially as it relates to movement. As Herbert Haze defined it in 1974, "Biomechanics is the study of the structure and function of biological systems by means of the methods of mechanics."[37]

The way nerves, muscles, bones, and organs work together to carry out movements is complicated, and an extensive knowledge of one's body is helpful in becoming a skilled basketball player. Simply dribbling a basketball or shooting a jump shot calls for every body part—from eyes to leg muscles—to work together.

Good Eyesight

Eyes are important to any athlete. They are especially important for basketball players, who have to take in many sights and process many visual images quickly to successfully pass the ball, catch the ball, shoot the ball, steal a pass, or run down the court. The part of the eye that takes in images is the retina, which is a complex, layered structure of tissues at the back of the eye. The retina contains cells that detect light and color. Visual images that the retina picks up trigger messages that travel through the optic nerve to the brain.

Six muscles around the outside of each eye work together to move the eye up and down and to coordinate the eyes so they move together. These muscles help the eyes focus, so they can see images clearly both near and far.

They also help players track images, or follow the ball and other teammates with their eyes.

Having two eyes that work together contributes to players' depth perception, or their ability to see the court in three dimensions and judge distances based on this. When the eyes send a picture of an object from two slightly different angles because they are located on two slightly different areas of the face, the brain is able to judge the distance to that object with a high degree of accuracy. With poor depth perception, players would have greater difficulty making baskets or completing passes because they could not easily determine how far they needed to throw the ball.

Some basketball players wear goggles to protect their eyes during games. They know that good vision is important for success on the court.

Court Vision

Peripheral vision—the ability to see things on the sides of the field of view while looking straight ahead—is so important in basketball that it has a special name: court vision. Court vision is the ability to see what is happening on the court, including at the edge of the field of vision. Players with good court vision are more aware of what is going on and can be ready to react more quickly than players with poor court vision.

Using court vision, players can avoid someone coming up on them from the side and can make last minute changes in passing to get the ball where they want it to be. Former Utah Jazz guard and Basketball Hall of Fame member John Stockton is an example of a basketball player with excellent court vision. Sportswriter Mark Welling recalled, "The vision which Stockton possessed seemed to be magical. He could find ways of fitting passes into non-existent passing lanes. Stockton was always three

Nerves and Neurons

The central nervous system—made up of the brain, spinal cord, and a network of nerves—governs the movement, balance, and coordination necessary to play basketball. The central nervous system is a complex system that passes chemical messages throughout the body, as explained by a writer for the Discovery Channel Kids website:

> *What are nerves? They're the thin threads of nerve cells, called neurons that run throughout your body ... All are shaped somewhat like flat stars which have, to varying degrees, been pulled at each end so that they have long fingers. The fingers of one neuron almost reach to the next neuron. When a neuron is stimulated—by heat, cold, touch, sound vibrations or some other message—it begins to actually generate a tiny electrical pulse. This electricity and chemical change travels the full length of the neuron. But when it gets to the end of finger-like points at the end of the neuron, it needs help getting across to the next extended finger. That's where chemicals come in. The electrical pulse in the cells triggers the release of chemicals that carry the pulse to the next cell. And so on and so on and so on.*[1]

1. "Your Nervous System," Discovery Kids. discoverykids.com/articles/your-nervous-system/.

or four steps ahead of the defenders."[38] Stockton's court vision was not magical, though. It was the product of natural physical ability being made even stronger by hard work and practice.

Hand-eye coordination is just as important as court vision. Hand-eye coordination is the ability of the brain to direct eyes and hands to work together to perform tasks such as catching a ball. It is based on the functioning of proprioceptors, which are specialized sensory receptors on nerve endings found in muscles, tendons, joints, and the inner ear. These receptors relay information about the body's motion or position.

Good hand-eye coordination allows players to quickly respond to stimuli, such as the ball coming at them or another player coming into their field of view. It also allows them to dribble quickly and skillfully. Stephen Curry is widely regarded as having excellent hand-eye coordination, and he practices it through drills designed to keep his eyes, hands, and central nervous system working at a high speed. As Steve Kerr, Curry's head coach with the Golden State Warriors, said, "The guy has the best hand-eye coordination of anybody I've ever seen."[39]

Fast Break!

Neurons can send signals to the brain at speeds that exceed 150 miles (241 km) per hour.

Balance in Basketball

Proprioceptors are also important in developing good balance, or the ability to remain stable despite changes in body position. Good balance is essential for playing basketball. It allows for power, control, and accuracy in shooting, dribbling, passing, and other moves. It is especially important to have good balance when pulling off difficult shots, such as a fadeaway jump shot. All basketball plays are more successful with good balance.

In addition to proprioceptors, the eyes and ears are involved in balance. The eyes function by giving the brain visual cues about whether the body is vertical, leaning in one direction, lying flat, or in some other position. The ears, specifically the inner ears, contain a fluid-filled system called the vestibular system, which is responsible for sensations of motion and balance. The Vestibular Disorders Association describes the vestibular system as such:

Sensory information about motion, equilibrium, and spatial orientation is provided by the vestibular apparatus, which in each ear includes the utricle, saccule, and three semicircular canals. The utricle and saccule detect gravity (information in a vertical orientation) and linear movement. The semicircular canals, which detect rotational movement, are located at right angles to each other and are filled with a fluid called endolymph. When the head rotates in the direction sensed by a particular canal, the endolymphatic fluid within it lags behind because of inertia, and exerts pressure against the canal's sensory receptor. The receptor then sends impulses to the brain about movement from the specific canal that is stimulated. When the vestibular organs on both sides of the head are functioning properly, they send symmetrical impulses to the brain. (Impulses originating from the right side are consistent with impulses originating from the left side.)[40]

A Stable Stance

A good stance, or physical position, while playing basketball goes a long way toward helping a player maintain good balance. The triple-threat position is standard in basketball because it allows players to be physically steady and ready to pass, dribble, or shoot instantaneously. Author Jon Oliver stated, "For Michael Jordan, effective use of the triple-threat position often resulted in his strongly taking the basketball to the basket and dunking with authority."[41]

In the triple-threat position, players crouch slightly so their center of gravity is closer to the floor. Center of gravity is the center of mass of an object, the point around which all weight is evenly distributed. Depending on how human beings position themselves, their center of gravity changes, with the center shifting to where the weight is most concentrated. The closer a basketball player's center of gravity is to the floor, the more stable they are, and the easier it is for them to maintain their balance.

In addition to a lower center of gravity, a larger base of support also increases stability. In the triple-threat position, players increase their base of support by placing their feet flat on the floor, about shoulder width apart, with one foot slightly ahead of the other. The head is slightly forward; the back is straight. Knees and elbows are bent and relaxed. In this position, potential energy is stored, ready to be used when legs and arms are straightened.

Shown here is an example of the triple-threat position. The player's low center of gravity helps him maintain his balance.

Fast Break!

Lisa Leslie was the first woman to dunk in a WNBA game.

When a basketball player sees their opponent attempt a shot, they often jump and put their hands up to block it without having to think about it. This is an example of a conditioned reflex.

Reflexes and Decisions

A stable stance helps basketball players prepare themselves to shoot, pass, or dribble, but how do basketball players know what to do with the ball once they have it? They use their reflexes. Without quick reflexes, players would not be able to make the lightning-fast pivots, throws, and catches that are common in basketball. They also would not be able to quickly assume the correct position to catch a ball that is thrown at them. Reflexes are automatic responses to stimuli, and players must not only have great innate reflexes, they must also have excellent conditioned reflexes. An innate reflex, such as blinking one's eyes, is instinctive. A person generally does not have to think about it. A conditioned reflex, such as catching a pass or jumping for a rebound, is learned. It becomes automatic only after much practice.

Players with quick reflexes have very short reaction times. Reaction time is the time it takes to respond after receiving a stimulus. It is generally fastest when only one logical response can be made. For example, when a person touches a hot stove, the first response is to pull away, and the move takes place in a fraction of a second.

When there is more than one possible response, however, reaction times may be longer. For instance, if a player has to decide whether to shoot or pass the ball, they have to think, even if only for a split second. Reaction time can be reduced if players know what to expect and are prepared to react to different stimuli in different situations. In basketball, knowing what to expect means understanding every aspect of the game extremely well. It also means studying opponents' moves and mannerisms. If players can train their body and brain to react quickly to situations on the court through intense, focused practice sessions for a long period of time, it will increase their chances of success. As sports training experts have stated, "Delays in responses can make the difference between winning and losing. Athletes who can accelerate the decision-making process have a competitive edge over their opponents."[42]

Handling the Ball

Ball-handling skills are the techniques basketball players use when they control the ball during the game. Good ball handling involves good hand-eye coordination, quick reflexes, and patience to practice until they master each technique. Players with the best skills are typically those who begin practicing them early in life, so they come naturally by the time they turn professional. Stephen Curry has some of the best ball-handling skills in the NBA. He has credited an ankle injury in 2012 with the development of his ball-handling skills. Since he could not put weight on his foot, he used to sit and practice moves, sometimes even using a tennis ball to improve his control. His hard work clearly paid off.

One of Curry's most famous ball-handling drills involves dribbling two basketballs at one time. ESPN staff writer Ethan Sherwood Strauss described it as "the basketball version of patting your head and rubbing your stomach at the same time."[43] This kind of drill forces the player to focus on multiple things simultaneously, preparing them for game situations that test multiple biomechanical abilities at once. By training the brain and body to become better at multitasking, these drills train players to think and act more quickly on the court. As Strauss stated, "[Ball handling] isn't purely about coordination; it's about multitasking. It's the ability to change speeds, directions and plans, all while running a play and attacking when holes open in the defense. Curry is able to dominate a sport as a smaller guard in part because he can do two things at once better than most larger men can do one."[44]

Ball-handling skills, like all examples of biomechanics in action, involve different parts of the body—from the brain to the hands to the feet—working together to create successful motion. Curry's training regimen pushes his biomechanical abilities to their limit

Stephen Curry's famous ball-handling skills were developed through practice using the latest knowledge of biomechanics and the most advanced technology.

using standard tools, such as tennis balls, and the latest technology. He has been willing to try new things to achieve greatness, and he is not the only basketball superstar using the most advanced technology to improve his skills.

Dribbling Drills

Stephen Curry is a master multitasker. Practicing his skills using two balls at once has helped him develop quick reflexes and decision-making capabilities. When visiting Curry on a typical training day in 2015, ESPN staff writer Ethan Sherwood Strauss described some of the drills Curry worked on, drills he was later called upon to try:

> *"Overload" means flooding your perception, to challenge your ability to focus on the tasks at hand. At its most basic representation, that's the idea behind Curry's now famous pregame dribbling drills. Dribbling two basketballs simultaneously is less a test of coordination than a test of realization ...*
>
> *Shortly into our conversations, I was put to the test ...*
>
> *Dribbling two basketballs at separate rhythms was tough, but workable. Quickly, life got much tougher. I was broken by one particular drill that involved dribbling between the legs while transferring another ball elsewhere ...*
>
> *There was the Steph drill where you catch a tennis ball while dribbling a basketball. There was the Steph drill where you dribble a heavy basketball and a regular one simultaneously. There was the drill that involved continuously transferring a ball to bounce between your legs while simultaneously maintaining a regular dribble with your other hand.*[1]

Each of these drills helps basketball players such as Curry learn to do many different tasks at one time. Curry and other professional players know that it is important to begin this kind of intense training with a coach or trainer who understands biomechanics.

1. Ethan Sherwood Strauss, "Training Day: How to Work Out Like Stephen Curry," ESPN, December 17, 2015. www.espn.com/nba/story/_/id/14378254/unorthodox-training-routine-golden-state-warriors-stephen-curry.

Chapter 7

The Future of the Game

Basketball has been played in the United States for more than 100 years, and, to some extent, little has changed about the sport since its earliest days. It still involves one ball and two baskets placed high above players' heads, and points are still scored by shooting the ball into the basket. However, when the change was made to move from peach baskets with the bottom still intact to nets that the ball falls through, the sport took an important step forward. The sport has continued to move forward from the time of Naismith to now, using the latest technology to make basketball safer, faster, and more fun to watch and to play.

As basketball players, coaches, and fans look to the future of the sport, they will see science being applied at every turn. Science and technology are changing the ways basketball players prepare for the game and recover after it is done. From practice methods to injury treatments, researchers and engineers are working hard to shape the future of basketball using the latest advances in science.

Success with Strobe Lights

Basketball players try many unusual training methods to improve their ball-handling skills. One such method involves wearing special goggles that use strobe light technology to flash between clear vision and darkness at different, adjustable speeds. Strobe lights have been used to help basketball players for years; Michael Jordan practiced with strobe lights to help him deal with the camera flashes and arena lighting effects that could distract him during foul shots or other important plays. Over time, it became clear that strobe lights could also be used to help players improve their court vision, hand-eye coordination, and reaction time.

Dr. Alan Reichow, who helped create one of the first pairs of strobe goggles used by basketball players, described the impact the technology has on athletes: "The general report by athletes is that it [the game] seems slower, it seems easier … Essentially what we've done is strength training on the sensory system. Just as you would with resistance training on the physical side, we're doing resistance training for the senses of the brain."[45] The flashing lights help basketball players develop better visual perception by initially making it more difficult to see. This trains the body and the brain to work harder to process and react to visual cues, which can have long-term benefits for reflexes and memory.

Neuroscientist Stephen Mitroff stated that he and his team of researchers discovered wearing strobe eyewear has another positive effect on basketball players: "We found improvements in anticipatory timing: being able to predict when a moving object is going to be at a certain spot."[46] This is incredibly helpful for basketball players, who need to be in exactly the right spot to accept passes, block shots, or dribble around other players.

This technology is still being studied to determine its complete benefits and drawbacks for all athletes, including basketball players. Strobe light goggles are still a rare sight in basketball training facilities, and only a select few players, including Stephen Curry, are known to use them on a regular basis. However, if more studies find that these goggles can improve player performance, strobe lights might be flashing in an increasing number of athletes' eyes.

LED Training

Strobe lights are not the only kind of lighting basketball players use in training. LED lighting has become a popular training tool for everything from hand-eye coordination and reaction time to specific footwork and passing drills. LED stands for light-emitting diode, which is a device that produces visible light when an electrical current passes through it. LEDs are good training tools because they emit light in a specific direction instead of other kinds of light bulbs, which emit light in all directions. This focused lighting and the fact that LEDs do not burn out in the same way traditional light bulbs do make them ideal to use in training situations.

There are many different LED training tools used by basketball players and other athletes. One training tool is a mat that can be put on the floor or on a wall with numbered circles lit by LEDs. By lighting the circles in different patterns at different speeds, players can practice dribbling and passing to specific points more quickly and accurately. Another

Laser Therapy

LEDs and other light sources are used for more than just athletic training. They are also used to treat injuries and help athletes deal with the pain that they experience after a game or tough training session. Some basketball players use a treatment method called low level light therapy, or low level laser therapy (LLLT), to help lessen the aches and pains that come with their sport. LLLT involves placing a low level laser, also known as a cold laser, or LED on the part of a person's body that is in pain or on specific pressure points similar to the Eastern practice of acupuncture. When certain wavelengths of light touch the body, they are believed to promote healing, ease swelling, and relieve pain. The results of LLLT are not long-lasting, but it does help athletes feel good enough to get back on the court and perform at their best soon after receiving the treatment.

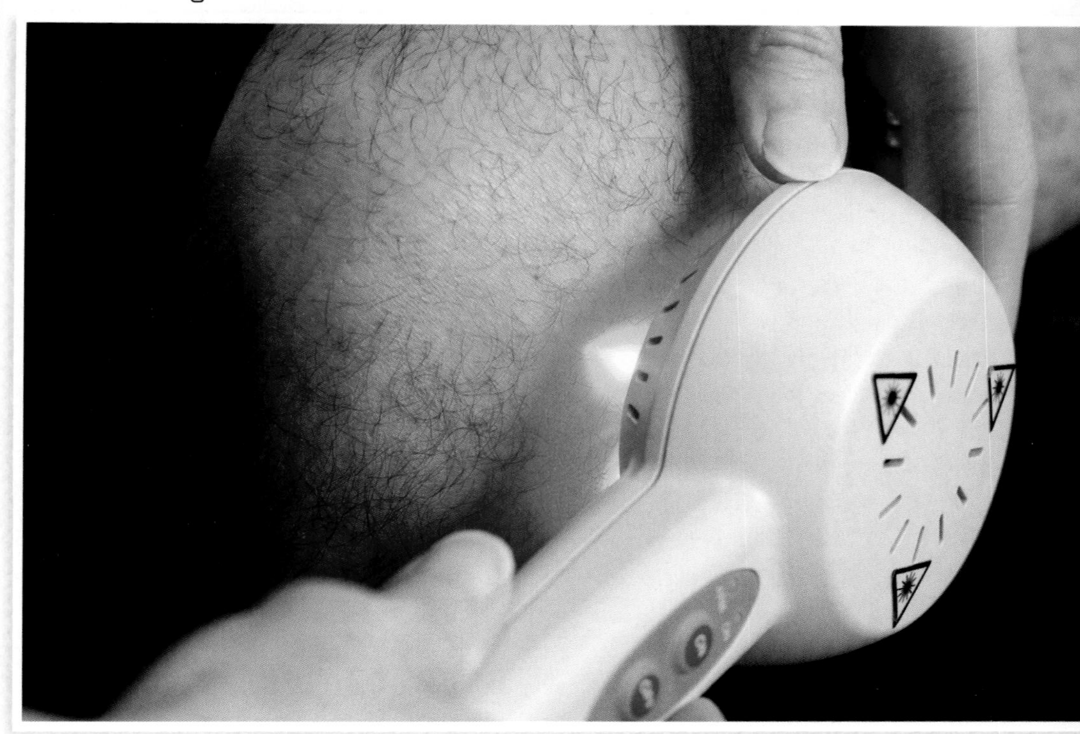

LLLT is used by basketball players because it is thought to be a relatively safe, drug-free, and fast way to ease pain and promote healing.

version of this technology uses small discs that are lit using LEDs, which can be placed on walls, floors, cones, or other objects or surfaces. These discs can be programmed to light in certain patterns at certain speeds, or a trainer or coach can control their lighting. The LEDs detect motion, so they turn off when a player runs over them, jumps over them, touches them, or passes their hand over them. These lights are used to improve basic basketball skills, such as coordination, agility, and speed. With some LED training systems, information about how quickly the lights were switched off and the targets were hit is sent to a computer or tablet, which allows players and coaches to easily evaluate the skills being worked on with these training tools.

One of the most advanced uses of LED technology is in the creation of full-size LED basketball courts. Nike created one in China in 2014, which was called the House of Mamba after NBA superstar Kobe Bryant's nickname, "Black Mamba." Another LED court was used to display the technology to visitors at the NBA All-Star Game in New York City in 2015. These LED courts were made using a wooden floor with a layer of LED screens on top protected by glass and a special surface that provides the friction necessary to play the sport safely and successfully.

LED basketball courts impress fans with their vibrant displays of changing colors and patterns, but they are meant to be used to train players in an immersive way. The LEDs create patterns on the court surface that players can follow for drills, and the whole court can be lit up to place athletes in specific game situations to practice plays. As journalist

LED basketball courts look cool, and they are also helpful training tools.

Stu Roberts explained, "Training exercises that the court can run include a sequence of fundamental skills drills, a test of shooting prowess from different spots on the court, dribbling drills and a defense drill using a digital defender."[47] Sensors in the court are also used to track players' movements as they follow the LED displays, which can provide important information on player performance. These courts look like they are from a science-fiction movie, but they are shaping the reality of basketball in new and exciting ways.

All in the Ball

Professional and college basketball players have teams of people who keep track of and calculate their statistics, or stats, which are pieces of data about their performance expressed in numbers. It can be difficult for players to keep track of their own stats, such as shots made and missed, especially during practice. To make this easier for players who do not have people assigned to monitor their stats, Wilson, a company that makes balls for a variety of sports, created the Wilson X Connected Basketball.

This "smart" basketball has a built-in sensor that keeps track of how many shots a player makes and misses. That information is then sent to a smartphone, so the player can view their stats, including total missed and made shots from different distances. There is also a simulated game that can be set up between a player and digital opponent, with the device keeping track of the score.

Fast Break!

As of 2017, Elena Delle Donne has a career free throw percentage of 93.83 percent. That means she makes almost 94 percent of the free throws she attempts. That is better than any other player in the WNBA or NBA.

Airtight Recovery

Basketball players are always looking for the best ways to help their muscles recover after a game or practice, and they often look to the latest technology to aid their recovery and keep them playing at the highest level. In recent years, air compression technology has been put to use on basketball players' bodies, and many NBA stars now swear by compression devices as the key to reducing muscle soreness and keeping their bodies in game shape.

LeBron James and Kevin Durant are just two of the big names in basketball who have helped popularize the use of air compression devices. These devices are placed on specific parts of the body, such as the legs, arms, or hips. When worn on the legs, they look like a thick pair of pants. Once the devices are in place, they inflate, or fill with air. That air is then used to compress and release the muscles in a pulsing pattern. This acts as a kind of massage, increasing the movement of fluid in the body after a workout and enhancing circulation.

Because air compression technology is so new in the field of sports medicine, more studies still need to be conducted to determine how effective it is. However, many basketball players and trainers believe these devices work wonders for sore muscles and can even be used in place of traditional warm-up exercises. An anonymous NBA trainer told the website Bleacher Report, "For that [warming up], they're just flat-out better [than traditional drills] … No one rolls an ankle. No one gets tired. Heck, it just feels good."[48]

These young athletes are using the same air compression devices that NBA stars use to recover from games and training sessions.

Analytics: The Science of Sports Stats

Just as science can be used to help people better understand basketball, math can also be a valuable subject when it comes to sports. Athletic performance is often expressed in numbers—from points scored to games played. This is especially true in basketball, in which stats are kept on everything from shooting percentage to assists and rebounds. In recent years, a growing field of study has emerged that uses these stats to predict whether a team or a player will be successful. As Terrance F. Ross described it in *The Atlantic*, "It's a revolution that's indisputably linked to the NBA's growing, but controversial, reliance on data to measure a team's likelihood of winning—a phenomenon vaguely defined as 'analytics.'"[1]

Analytics experts use stats to compare teams and players to plan game strategies, such as determining whether or not a team should try to shoot more three-point shots against a certain opponent based on their shooting percentage and their opponent's previous defensive stats. They also use analytics to evaluate players based on mathematical facts.

Some fans, coaches, general managers, and retired players have openly stated their dislike of analytics. They believe players should be evaluated solely based on gut instinct and what can be seen during a game and in practice. They also fear that analytics could make the sport seem robotic. As Ross stated, "What happens when every team is employing the same strategies deemed to be the most effective? Does it take all the unpredictability—the magic—out of the sport?"[2]

However, many people involved in professional basketball today—from owners and players to fans and broadcasters—see analytics as a way of making the sport even better. Writer Kirk Goldsberry voiced this opinion by stating, "People say that analytics are taking the fun out of it, I think the NBA is in a better position now than it's ever been."[3] No matter which side of the analytics debate people fall on, they cannot ignore that math is becoming increasingly important in the world of basketball.

1. Terrance F. Ross, "Welcome to Smarter Basketball," *The Atlantic*, June 25, 2015. www.theatlantic.com/entertainment/archive/2015/06/nba-data-analytics/396776/.
2. Ross, "Welcome to Smarter Basketball."
3. Quoted in Ross, "Welcome to Smarter Basketball."

The Deep Freeze Debate

Another futuristic recovery method some NBA players, including James, have tried is cryotherapy, which is an extreme version of using ice to treat injuries and muscle soreness. Instead of placing an ice pack on a sore body part or even soaking in an ice bath as some athletes do, those who go through cryotherapy sessions put their body in a chamber that is blasted with liquid nitrogen, which creates temperatures that can reach as low as −300 degrees Fahrenheit (−184.4 degrees Celsius). A basketball player remains in the chamber for two to three minutes. During this time, the body goes into survival mode, and the blood rushes to protect the vital organs. Then, when the athlete gets out of the chamber, the blood rushes to the rest of the body, which is believed to help muscles recover and to help heal injured body parts.

Athletes from many sports around the world are turning to cryotherapy to help them deal with injuries and muscle soreness.

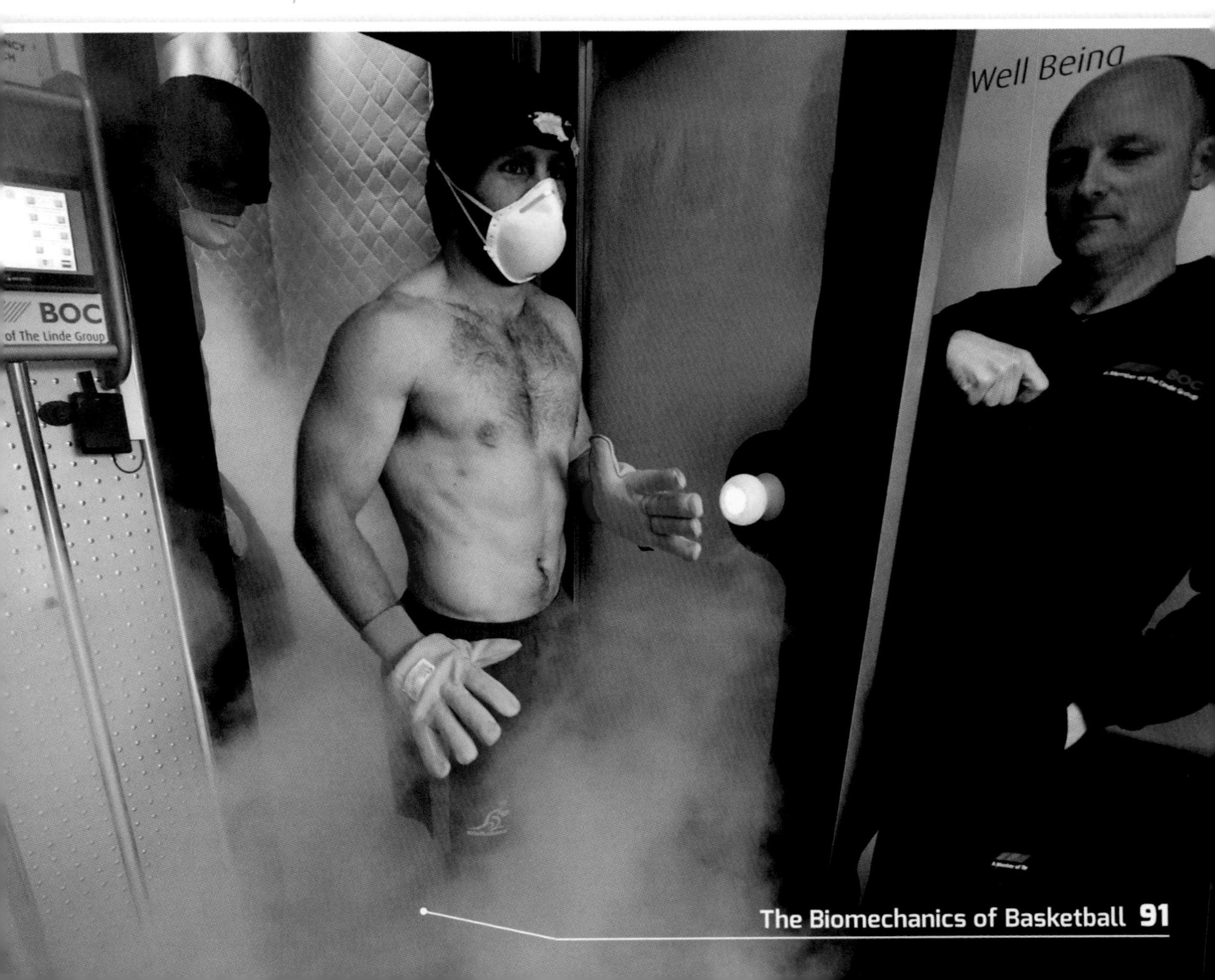

Many NBA players use cryotherapy, and some teams even have cryotherapy chambers in their training rooms. However, not everyone believes this is a beneficial treatment for every athlete. Journalist Mary Schmitt Boyer described the following in an article about the Cleveland Cavaliers and their use of cryotherapy:

> *Former Cavs trainer Max Benton … isn't convinced, either. He thinks a large part of the benefit is psychological.*
>
> *"I think it's just a short-term recovery," said Benton, now an athletic trainer at Southwest General Hospital who also works with athletes at Olmsted Falls High School. "There's so many different aspects to health care. For some people it works. For some people it doesn't. If it doesn't hurt you, if you feel like it's benefiting you, then I don't see any harm in it.*[49]

One group that does see potential harm in cryotherapy, though, is the U.S. Food and Drug Administration (FDA). In a 2016 report about the treatment method, medical experts stated that there was not enough evidence to support the use of cryotherapy. The report also listed health problems that could be associated with cryotherapy sessions:

> *Potential hazards include asphyxiation, especially when liquid nitrogen is used for cooling … The addition of nitrogen vapors to a closed room lowers the amount of oxygen in the room and can result in hypoxia, or oxygen deficiency, which could lead the user to lose consciousness. Moreover, subjects run the risk of frostbite, burns, and eye injury from the extreme temperatures.*[50]

Although some experts argue against subjecting the body to such cold temperatures, many basketball players claim they have seen improvement in how their body feels when they spend time in a cryotherapy chamber after a game.

Running Without Gravity

One piece of technology used to help basketball players recover from an injury was actually developed by scientists from the National Aeronautics and Space Administration (NASA) to help astronauts exercise in space. These scientists wanted to create a treadmill that astronauts could run on without floating away or being held in place by an uncomfortable harness, so they developed one that held a person in place using air pressure.

This kind of treadmill inflates with air to create a vacuum around the person running on it. The vacuum removes the strain of gravity on the runner and takes on a large percentage of their body weight, instead of placing that weight on their joints. This was helpful for astronauts, but it was also clear that it could be used to help athletes recover from injuries to their lower body. By reducing the stress that comes from gravity on an athlete's lower body as they run, this treadmill allows athletes to begin working out sooner after being hurt because their body is under less strain. Because the person on the treadmill is under less physical stress, they can focus more on running with good form and retraining their body to perform as it did before it was injured. This antigravity technology was pushed into the sports spotlight when Bryant used it while recovering from an Achilles tendon injury.

Treadmills that remove the force of gravity on joints look futuristic but are being used in the present to help athletes recover from injuries and stay in shape.

Fast Break!

An antigravity treadmill can reduce the stress of gravity on a runner's body by as much as 80 percent.

Focused on the Future

In February 2017, the NBA announced a new partnership with the Gatorade Sports Science Institute (GSSI). Through this partnership, the NBA's development league, now known as the G-League, became the testing ground for new studies by the GSSI. Under this agreement, G-League players would serve as the subjects of scientific studies on nutrition and the relationship between nutrients, the human body, and physical activity.

This partnership between the NBA and a leading sports science research institute shows that basketball and science will continue to be linked far into the future. As new technologies are developed and the relationship between science and sports is pushed into new and exciting places, basketball players will become faster, stronger, and safer on the court.

Science and technology are being used to shape the exciting future of basketball.

Notes

Chapter 1:
From Humble Beginnings to Worldwide Fame

1 Quoted in Michael Levenson and Andrew Ryan, "Hoop Heaven," *The Boston Globe*, June 20, 2008. archive.boston.com/news/local/articles/2008/06/20/hoop_heaven/?page=full.

2. Quoted in Kansas Historical Society, "James Naismith," Kansaspedia, January 2016. www.kshs.org/kansapedia/james-naismith/12154.

3. Quoted in Robert W. Peterson, *Cages to Jump Shots: Basketball's Early Years*. New York, NY: Oxford University Press, 1990, p. 21.

4. Quoted in Peterson, *Cages to Jump Shots*, p. 20.

5. Senda Berenson Abbot, "Basket Ball at Smith College." *Spalding's Athletic Library*, c. 1914, pp. 69–77. clio.fivecolleges.edu/smith/berenson/5pubs/bball_smith/index.shtml?page=4.

6. Quoted in Peterson, *Cages to Jump Shots*, pp. 46–47.

7. Quoted in Peterson, *Cages to Jump Shots*, p. 107.

8. Quoted in Richard Sandomir, "After Two Decades, W.N.B.A. Still Struggling for Relevance," *New York Times*, May 28, 2016. www.nytimes.com/2016/05/28/sports/basketball/after-two-decades-wnba-still-struggling-for-relevance.html.

Chapter 2:
Training for Results

9. Steven M. Traina, "NBA Players Always in Training," ESPN, September 2, 2007. espn.go.com/trainingroom/s/fitness/index.html.

10. Traina, "NBA Players Always in Training."

11. Jerry Tarkanian, "Basketball Shooting Is Both Art and Science," Coach Like a Pro, 2013. www.coachlikeapro.com/basketball-shooting.html.

12. Quoted in Gilbert Rogin, "We Are Grown Men Playing a Child's Game," *Sports Illustrated*, November 18, 1963. www.si.com/vault/1963/11/18/594385/we-are-grown-men-playing-a-childs-game.

13. Goran Markovic, "Does Plyometric Training Improve Vertical Jump Height? A Meta-Analytical Review," U.S. National Library of Medicine, March 8, 2007. www.ncbi.nlm.nih.gov/pmc/articles/PMC2465309/.
14. NBA.com Staff, "Joakim Noah Apologizes to Fans, Knicks for 20-Game Suspension," NBA.com, March 28, 2017. www.nba.com/article/2017/03/28/knicks-joakim-noah-apologizes-suspension.
15. Kevin Draper, "NBA Bans O. J. Mayo for Violating Anti-Drug Program," Deadspin, July 1, 2016. deadspin.com/nba-bans-o-j-mayo-for-violating-anti-drug-program-1782965570.
16. Quoted in "Anabolic Steroids," ESPN, September 6, 2007. espn.go.com/special/s/drugsandsports/steroids.html.

Chapter 3: Injuries: Sidelining Star Athletes

17. Dan Bell, "Keeping Them Fine-Tuned," NBA.com, 2014. www.nba.com/timberwolves/news/Keeping_Them_FineTuned-300855-1193.html.
18. Quoted in Baxter Holmes, "Kobe Bryant Plays in Lakers' Loss After Trainer Pops Finger Back In," ESPN, February 20, 2016. www.espn.com/nba/story/_/id/14811159/kobe-bryant-plays-dislocating-finger-los-angeles-lakers-loss.
19. Robert H. Shmerling, "The Gender Gap in Sports Injuries," Harvard Health Publications, December 3, 2015. www.health.harvard.edu/blog/the-gender-gap-in-sports-injuries-201512038708.
20. Christine Aschwanden, "Women Get Sports Concussions at Higher Rates Than Men," FiveThirtyEight, May 17, 2016. fivethirtyeight.com/features/women-get-sports-concussions-at-higher-rates-than-men/.
21. Quoted in Jonathan Feigen, "Yao on Season-Ending Injury: 'It's Better Than Last Year,'" *Houston Chronicle*, May 10, 2009. www.chron.com/sports/rockets/article/Yao-on-season-ending-injury-It-s-better-than-1723812.php.
22. Quoted in Tom Callahan, "Beyond the Traditional in Sports Medicine," *New York Times*, May 10, 1998. www.nytimes.com/1998/05/10/nyregion/beyond-the-traditional-in-sports-medicine.html.
23. Rick Wilson, "Arthroscopy," American Academy of Orthopaedic Surgeons, May 2010. orthoinfo.aaos.org/topic.cfm?topic=a00109.

24. Quoted in Matt Norlander, "Arizona's Ray Smith, Only 19, Leaving Basketball After Third ACL Injury," CBS Sports, November 3, 2016. www.cbssports.com/college-basketball/news/arizonas-ray-smith-only-19-leaving-basketball-after-third-acl-injury/.

Chapter 4: Gear for the Game

25. Tim Newcomb, "Stepping Softly: Getting to the Bottom of Basketball Sneaker Cushioning," *Sports Illustrated*, April 3, 2015. www.si.com/nba/2015/04/03/investigating-sneaker-cushioning-nike-adidas-jordan.

Chapter 5: Physics and Basketball

26. Aatish Bhatia, "Galileo Got Game: 5 Things You Didn't Know About the Physics of Basketball," *Wired*, April 23, 2014. www.wired.com/2014/04/basketball-physics/.
27. David Watson, "The First Law of Thermodynamics with Examples," FT Exploring Science and Technology, 2014. www.ftexploring.com/energy/first-law.html.
28. "In Basketball, Shooting Angle Has a Big Effect on the Chances of Scoring," *Washington Post*, March 16, 2010. www.washingtonpost.com/wp-dyn/content/article/2010/03/15/AR2010031502017.html.
29. Quoted in Mick Kulikowski, "The Physics of Free Throws," North Carolina State University. www.ncsu.edu/bulletin/archive/2009/11/11-12/freethrow.php.
30. John J. Fontanella, *The Physics of Basketball*. Baltimore, MD: Johns Hopkins University Press, 2006, p. 80.
31. Bhatia, "Galileo Got Game."
32. Kulikowski, "The Physics of Free Throws."
33. Quoted in Ira Berkow, ed., *Court Vision: Unexpected Views on the Lure of Basketball*. New York, NY: Harper Collins, 2000, p. 72.
34. Bhatia, "Galileo Got Game."
35. Science Buddies, "Surface Science: Where Does a Basketball Bounce Best?," *Scientific American*, May 1, 2014. www.scientificamerican.com/article/surface-science-where-does-a-basketball-bounce-best/.
36. "Basketball Rebounding: Eight Qualities for Success," Ultimate-Youth-Basketball-Guide.com, 2017. www.ultimate-youth-basketball-guide.com/basketball-rebounding.html.

Chapter 6: The Biomechanics of Basketball

37. Quoted in Peter M. McGinnis, *Biomechanics of Sport and Exercise, Second Edition.* Champaign, IL: Human Kinetics, 2005, p. 3.
38. Mark Welling, "The Definition of a True NBA Point Guard—Why I Love John Stockton's Game," Bleacher Report, September 22, 2009. bleacherreport.com/articles/259291-marks-thoughts-why-i-love-john-stocktons-game.
39. Quoted in Rusty Simmons, "Stephen Curry's Hand-Eye Coordination Is a Marvel," SFGate, April 5, 2016. www.sfgate.com/warriors/article/Steph-Curry-s-hand-eye-coordination-is-a-marvel-7227761.php.
40. "The Human Balance System," Vestibular Disorders Association. vestibular.org/understanding-vestibular-disorder/human-balance-system.
41. Jon Oliver, *Basketball Fundamentals; A Better Way to Learn the Basics.* Champaign, IL: Human Kinetics Publishers, 2004, p. 2.
42. "Sports Training Tips to Improve Reaction Time and Decision Making," Team Sport Guide, July 28, 2010. www.teamsportguide.com/sports-training-tips-to-improve-reaction-time-and-decision-making/.
43. Ethan Sherwood Strauss, "Training Day: How to Work Out Like Stephen Curry," ESPN, December 17, 2015. www.espn.com/nba/story/_/id/14378254/unorthodox-training-routine-golden-state-warriors-stephen-curry.
44. Strauss, "Training Day."

Chapter 7: The Future of the Game

45. Quoted in Tom Haberstroh, "How Did Kawhi Leonard—and Steph Curry—Train Their Brains? Strobe Lights (Yes, Really)," ESPN, November 9, 2016. www.espn.com/nba/story/_/id/18002545/kawhi-leonard-strobe-light-training-nba.
46. Quoted in Drake Bennett, "Nike's Strobe-Light Glasses Prove Helpful. Good Luck Finding Them," *Bloomberg*, December 18, 2013. www.bloomberg.com/news/articles/2013-12-18/nikes-strobe-light-glasses-prove-helpful-dot-good-luck-finding-them.
47. Stu Roberts, "Nike Created LED Motion-Tracking Basketball Court," New Atlas, August 22, 2014. newatlas.com/nike-house-of-mamba-basketball-court/33437/.

48. Quoted in Will Carroll, "NBA's Wonderful Toys: The Technology Used in NBA Training Rooms," Bleacher Report, November 21, 2103. bleacherreport.com/articles/1857081-nbas-wonderful-toys-the-technology-used-in-nba-training-rooms.
49. Mary Schmitt Boyer, "The Cold Hard Truth About Cryotherapy: NBA Insider," Cleveland.com, January 19, 2014. www.cleveland.com/cavs/index.ssf/2014/01/the_cold_hard_truth_about_cryo.html.
50. Quoted in "Whole Body Cryotherapy (WBC): A 'Cool' Trend that Lacks Evidence, Poses Risks," U.S. Food and Drug Administration, July 5, 2016. www.fda.gov/ForConsumers/ConsumerUpdates/ucm508739.htm

Glossary

arc: A curved path.

cartilage: A tough, flexible tissue that makes up some body parts, such as the nose and outer ear.

central nervous system: The parts of the brain and spinal cord that receive and process stimuli from the body and coordinate appropriate physical responses.

concussion: Injury to the brain caused by a blow, a fall, or violent shaking.

endurance: The ability to tolerate difficult physical activity for a long period of time.

energy: The ability to do work.

estrogen: A hormone that naturally occurs in the body. Women have higher levels than men.

hyperextend: To extend so the angle between the bones of a joint is greater than normal.

lactic acid: An acid made by muscles during strenuous exercise.

mass: The measurement of an object's size and how much matter it contains.

projectile: An object that, once started by a force, continues in motion by its own inertia and is influenced only by the downward force of gravity.

rugby: A football sport in which forward passing is not allowed but kicking, dribbling, backward passing, and tackling are allowed.

stimulus: An event or condition in the environment that directly influences bodily activity in a living thing.

wavelength: The distance in the line of advance of a wave from any one point to the next corresponding point.

For More Information

Books

Buckley, James Jr. *STEM in Sports: Math.* Broomall, PA: Mason Crest, 2015.
This book introduces readers to the importance of math as it relates to sports, as well as its relationship to the other areas of STEM: science, technology, and engineering.

Chandler, Matt. *The Science of Basketball: The Top Ten Ways Science Affects the Game.* North Mankato, MN: Capstone Press, 2016.
Chandler's list of the most important examples of science in basketball presents a creative look at this topic.

Goodstein, Madeline P. *Sports Science Fair Projects.* New York, NY: Enslow Publishing, 2016.
Basic experiments give readers a hands-on sense of the science behind a variety of sports, including basketball.

Graubart, Norman D. *The Science of Basketball.* New York, NY: PowerKids Press, 2016.
This book provides readers with a basic overview of how physics is applied to the sport of basketball.

Stuckey, Rachel. *Full Court Press: Basketball Skills and Drills.* New York, NY: Crabtree Publishing, 2016.
Stuckey details a number of common basketball drills to help aspiring players improve their technique and performance.

Yomtov, Nelson. *Being Your Best at Basketball.* New York, NY: Children's Press, 2017.
Yomtov gives readers an overview of the basic rules of basketball and tips for training to be a successful player on the court.

Websites

"Galileo Got Game: 5 Things You Didn't Know About the Physics of Basketball"
www.wired.com/2014/04/basketball-physics
This article from *Wired* magazine highlights five detailed examples of how physics concepts can be applied to basketball.

NBA
www.nba.com
The official website of the NBA allows fans to learn more about the sport of basketball and its current teams and players through statistics, photos, videos, and articles.

Safety Tips: Basketball
kidshealth.org/en/teens/safety-basketball.html
This TeensHealth page provides visitors with information on basic basketball safety, including what gear to wear and how to prevent injuries.

"Surface Science: Where Does a Basketball Bounce Best?"
www.scientificamerican.com/article/surface-science-where-does-a-basketball-bounce-best/
This *Scientific American* article presents a detailed experiment young people can use to determine which surface allows a basketball to bounce best.

USA Basketball
www.usab.com
The official website of USA Basketball allows visitors to learn about the U.S. national basketball teams for men and women, as well as development leagues for younger players. Helpful tips for young players are also provided, including articles about using science to perfect skills.

WNBA
www.wnba.com
The WNBA's official website includes information on the league's history and its current players. Visitors can read articles about, see photos of, and watch videos featuring the top women in professional basketball.

Index

A

Abbott, Senda Berenson, 9
Abdul-Jabbar, Kareem, 14
acceleration, 60–62
Achilles tendinitis, 40
Ackerman, Val, 16
Adidas, 54
African Americans
    integrated teams, 13
    segregated teams, 12
    See also specific players
agility, 13, 19, 21, 45, 86
alcohol, 27
All American Red Heads, 10
Alzheimer's disease, 38–39
Amateur Athletic Union (AAU), 11
ambidexterity, 23
American Academy of Orthopaedic Surgeons, 45
amphetamines, 29
anabolic steroids, 29–31
analytics, 90
angles
    in dribbling, 71
    of incidence, 71
    rebound from basket and, 67
    of reflection, 71
    in shooting, 63–68
anterior cruciate ligament (ACL), 36–37, 46
antigravity treadmill, 92–94
anti-inflammatory medicines, 42
antimicrobial fabrics, 54
applied force, defined, 61
arthroscopic surgery, 45
Auriemma, Geno, 15

B

backboards, 10, 13, 67, 70
backspin, 67–68
bacteria, 54
balance, 21, 38, 73, 76–78
balls
    energy transference between players and, 72
    handling skills, 80–81, 83
    history, 51
    inflation, 47, 51–52
    Spalding, 51
    trajectory, 62, 64, 68, 70
barnstormers, 10–12
Barry, Rick, 62
base of support, 76
Baylor, Elgin, 13
Beasley, Michael, 23
Bird, Larry, 14
biomechanics, defined, 74
Black Fives, 12
blocking
    as conditioned reflex, 79
    defined, 10
Boston Celtics, 6, 48
brain, 21, 33, 38–39, 74–78, 80, 84

broken bones, 32–35, 40–42, 45–46, 48
bruises, 32–33, 39, 42, 46
Bryant, Kobe
Achilles tendon injury, 83
ambidexterity and, 23
"Black Mamba" nickname, 86
finger injury, 36

C

calories, 25
Canada, 8
carbohydrates, 26–27
cardiac muscles, 19
center of gravity, 78
central nervous system, 16, 23, 77
Chamberlain, Wilt, 13
Charged Cushioning (Under Armour), 57
charging, 10
China, 86
chronic injuries
Achilles tendinitis, 40
defined, 32
patellar tendinitis, 39–40
stress fractures, 40–41, 48
chronic traumatic encephalopathy (CTE), 39
clap push-ups, 23
Cleveland Cavaliers, 27, 92
coaches, 17, 39, 42, 82–83, 86, 90
cocaine, 29
cold lasers, 85
college teams
development of, 13–16
first women's, 9
March Madness, 6, 13, 34
composite basketballs, 51
compound fractures, 33–35
compression devices, 88–89
compression sleeves, 53
computerized tomography scans (CT scans), 42
concussions, 33, 38–39, 54
conditioned reflexes, 79
contusions. *See* bruises
Converse All Star shoes, 54, 55
Cooper, Chuck, 13
corticosteroids, 44
cortisone, 44
court dimensions, 49–50
court surfaces, 47–49, 51, 86
court vision, 76–77, 84
creatine, 28
crossover play, 11, 22
cryotherapy, 91–92
Curry, Stephen, 14, 16–17, 23, 37, 57, 77, 80–82, 84

D

dehydration, 26
Delayed Onset Muscle Soreness (DOMS), 20
Delle Donne, Elena, 16, 88
dental injuries, 54
depth perception, 75
Diggins, Skylar, 14
dribbling, 10–12, 21–23, 71, 74, 77–80, 82, 84, 87
drugs of abuse (NBA definition), 29
Durant, Kevin, 17, 37, 88

E

energy
- in dribbling, 71
- and physics, 57–58
- in shooting, 61
- transference between player and ball, 72
- types, 59–61

enzymes, 26
ethylene vinyl acetate (EVA), 56
eyes
- balance and, 77
- coordination with hands, 77, 80, 84
- depth perception and, 75
- muscles of, 74
- peripheral vision, 76
- retina, 74

F

fadeaway jump shot, 13, 77
fast-twitch muscle fibers, 19–20
fat, 26–27, 43
finger dislocations, 36
force, defined, 61
fouls, 8, 10
fractures. *See* broken bones
free throws, 66–67, 88
friction
- defined, 54, 67
- and safety, 54

G

Gatorade Sports Science Institute (GSSI), 94
gender comparisons
- ACL problems, 37
- concussions, 38
- stress fractures, 41

G-League, 94
goggles
- for safety, 75
- for strobe light training, 83–84

Golden State Warriors, 37, 77
"granny shots," 62–63
gravity
- center of, 78
- dribbling and, 71
- shooting and, 62, 67–68

H

half-reverse dribble, 11
hang time, 68–70
Harlem Globetrotters, 12
Harlem Rens, 12
head fake play, 13
hemoglobin, 26
heroin, 29
hertz, defined, 68
history
- balls, 51
- courts, 47–48
- equipment, 47
- Naismith and, 6–10
- shoes, 54–55
- uniforms, 52, 54
- women, 9–10, 13, 16

hoops
- changes, 10–11, 83
- original (peach baskets), 7, 10, 83
- peach baskets replaced, 10, 83

House of Mamba, 86
human growth hormone (HGH), 29
hydration, 26
hydrocortisone, 44

I

inertia, 60, 62, 64
inflation of balls, 47, 51–52
injuries
acute, 32–39, 42, 45
career-ending, 45–46
chronic, 32, 39–45
dental, 54
diagnosing, 39, 42–43
dislocations, 32, 36
head. *See* concussions
knee, 36–37, 39–40
playing through pain, 36
strains and sprains, 33, 35–37, 39, 42
treatment for
physical therapy, 45
P.R.I.C.E. method, 42
surgery, 33, 35, 37, 42, 45
innate reflexes, 79
integration, 13
International Basketball Federation (FIBA), 17, 49
Iverson, Allen, 53

J

James, LeBron, 17, 23, 88, 91
joints, 21, 32, 35–37, 45, 48, 77, 92–93
Jordan, Michael, 14
ambidexterity, 23
hang time, 68–69
height of jumps, 68
strobe light training, 83
triple-threat stance, 78
jumper's knee, 39–40
jumpshots, 13, 20, 23, 34, 57, 65, 74, 77

K

Kerr, Steve, 77
kinetic energy, 60–61, 71–72
knee injuries, 36–37, 39–40

L

lactic acid, 20
lateral collateral ligament (LCL), 36
law of conservation of energy, 59–60
law of inertia, 60
law of reflection, 71
Leslie, Lisa, 79
light-emitting diodes (LEDs)
full-size court with, 86–87
as injury treatment, 85
as training tool, 84, 86–87
low level light therapy (LLLT), 85

M

magnetic resonance imaging (MRI), 42–43
Major League Baseball, 38
March Madness, 6, 13, 34
marijuana, 29
massage, 20, 45, 88

math, 50–51, 60, 90
Mayo, O.J., 29
medial collateral ligament (MCL), 36–37
medicines, 20, 42
memory loss, 38–39
microfibers, 54
Miller, Sean, 46
Moore, Maya, 14
morphine, 29
mouth guards, 54
muscle memory, 21–22
muscles
 of eyes, 74
 fiber types, 19–20
 skeletal, defined, 19
 sore, 20
 types, 19
myocytes, 91

N
Naismith, James, 6–10, 83
Naismith Memorial Basketball Hall of Fame, 10, 81
Naismith Trophy, 17
National Aeronautics and Space Administration (NASA), 92
National Basketball Association (NBA)
 championships, 6
 concussion protocol, 39
 court dimensions, 49, 50
 founded, 13
 growth, 16–17
 integration, 13
 substance abuse policy, 29
National Basketball League, 11
National Collegiate Athletic Association (NCAA), 13, 15, 28, 34–35, 49
National Football League, 38–39
National Hockey League, 38
National Institute on Drug Abuse, 30–31
neurons, 76–77
New York Renaissance. *See* Harlem Rens
New York Wanderers, 11
Newton, Isaac, 60–62
Newton's laws of motion, 60–62, 67, 71
Nike, 54, 86
Noah, Joakim, 28–29
nutrition, 26–28, 94

O
offseason fitness, 18
Olson, C.M., 10
O'Neal, Shaquille, 56
Onuaku, Chinanu, 62–63
orthotics, 56
overuse injuries. *See* chronic injuries

P
pain-relieving medicines, 20, 42
parabolic path, 62, 64, 68, 70
Parker, Candace, 23
passing, 8, 72–80, 84
patellar tendinitis. *See* jumper's knee
Paul, Chris, 14
peach baskets, 7, 10, 83
performance-enhancing substances, 28–31

Phylon, 56
physical therapy, 45
physics, defined, 56, 58
players
with career-ending injuries, 45–46
energy transference between balls and, 72
height of, 13, 40, 68
See also specific individuals
plyometric drills, 23–25
polyurethane, 56
popularity
All American Red Heads, 10
college basketball, 6, 13–14
commercialization and, 17
posterior cruciate ligament (PCL), 36–37
potential energy, 60–61, 71, 78
power skips, 23–24
prednisone, 44
P.R.I.C.E. treatment, 42
projectile, defined, 62
proprioception, 21
protein, 19, 26–28, 39

R
ray, defined, 65
reaction time, 23, 79–80, 84
reflection, 67
reflexes, 79–80, 82, 84
Reichow, Alan, 84
release angle, defined, 65
repeated concussions, 39
rhythm, 82
Robertson, Oscar, 13
rules, 8–10
running bank shot, 13
running with ball (traveling), 10
Russell, Bill
height, 13
on work required to make moves automatic, 22

S
Savoy Big Five. *See* Harlem Globetrotters
segregation, 12
shin splints, 39
shock training. *See* plyometric drills
shoes
anatomy, 55–56
Converse All Stars, 54–55
history, 54–55
materials, 56–57
shooting
backspin, 67–68
energy involved, 61
muscle memory and, 21, 22
path of ball, 62, 64, 68, 70
"shooting short," 67
shoulder dislocations, 36
Shumpert, Iman, 27
simple sugars, 27
skeletal muscles, 19
slam dunks, 24–25, 57–58, 68, 70
slow-twitch muscle fibers, 19, 20
"smart" basketballs, 88
smartphones, 88
Smith College, 9
Smith, Ray, 45–46
smooth muscles, 19
sneakers. *See* shoes
soft hands, 72–73

sore muscles. *See* Delayed Onset Muscle Soreness (DOMS)
Spalding basketballs, 51
speed training, 20
sprained ankles, 35
statistics, 88, 90
steroids. *See* anabolic steroids and corticosteroids
Stockton, John, 76–77
strains and sprains, 33, 35–37, 39, 42
strength training, 20–21
stress fractures, 40–41, 48
strobe light training, 83–84
supplements, 28–29
surgery, 33, 35, 37, 42, 45

T

Taurasi, Diana, 14
Taylor, Charles H. "Chuck," 54
teams
- early professional, 11
- integrated, 13
- numbers of players on, 8, 10
- segregated, 12
- YMCAs, 11

technology, 42, 60, 81, 83–84, 88, 94
tendinitis, 39–40
timing, 84
Title IX (Title Nine), 15
training
- agility, 21
- fast-twitch muscle fibers, 19–20
- slow-twitch muscle fibers, 19–20
- speed, 20
- strength, 20–21
- year-round, 18

trajectory, 62, 64, 68, 70
treatment of injuries
- physical therapy, 45
- P.R.I.C.E. method, 42
- surgery, 33, 35, 37, 42, 45

triple-threat stance, 78

U

Under Armour, 57
uniforms, 52, 54
University of Connecticut Huskies, 15
U.S. Food and Drug Administration (FDA), 92

V

velocity, 60
Verkhoshansky, Yuri, 23
vertex, defined, 65
vertical jump, 24–25, 68
vestibular system, 77–78

W

Wade, Dwyane, 14
Ware, Kevin, 34–35
water therapy, 45
Webb, Spudd, 68
weight lifting as therapy, 45
Wilson X Connected Basketball, 88
Wilt, Fred, 23
women
- history of participation in basketball, 9, 10, 13, 16
- injuries, 37–38, 41
- uniforms, 52, 54

Women's National Basketball Association (WNBA), 16, 23, 28, 45, 48–49, 51, 79, 88
World Cup, FIBA, 17

X
X-rays, 42

Y
Yao Ming, 40, 41
YMCAs, 7, 11, 12

Picture Credits

Cover, pp. 37, 75 Aspen Photo/Shutterstock.com; cover, pp. 1, 3, 4, 6, 18, 32, 47, 58, 74, 83, 95, 100, 101, 103, 111, 112, back cover (background) Ekaterina Koolaeva/Shutterstock.com; pp. 4, 6, 18, 32, 47, 58, 74, 83 (basketball icon) tmicons/Shutterstock.com; p. 8 Tom Herde/The Boston Globe via Getty Images; p. 9 Kirn Vintage Stock/Corbis via Getty Images; pp. 12, 22, 44 Ethan Miller/Getty Images; pp. 14, 63 Andy Lyons/Getty Images; p. 15 Jamie Sabau/Getty Images; pp. 16, 81, 94 Ezra Shaw/Getty Images; p. 19 Andy Cross/The Denver Post via Getty Images; pp. 24–25 Bob Donnan-Pool/Getty Images; p. 26 Thearon W. Henderson/Getty Images; p. 27 Jason Miller/Getty Images; p. 28 Jim McIsaac/Getty Images; p. 33 Gene Sweeney Jr/Getty Images; p. 34 Mike Ehrmann/Getty Images; pp. 40–41, 53 John W. McDonough/Sports Illustrated/Getty Images; p. 43 zlikovec/Shutterstock.com; p. 48 Greg Nelson/Sports Illustrated/Getty Images; p. 50 Es sarawuth/Shutterstock.com; p. 51 Bettmann/Contributor/Getty Images; p. 52 George Rinhart/Corbis via Getty Images; p. 55 emka74/Shutterstock.com; p. 59 Erick W. Rasco/Sports Illustrated/Getty Images; p. 61 Everett Historical/Shutterstock.com; p. 64 oneinchpunch/Shutterstock.com; p. 66 Shelley Lipton/Icon Sportswire via Getty Images; p. 69 JEFF HAYNES/AFP/Getty Images; pp. 72–73 Harry How/Getty Images; p. 78 Cal Sports Media via AP Images; p. 79 Jonathan Daniel/Getty Images; p. 85 Jim Craigmyle/Corbis/Getty Images; pp. 86–87 Timothy Hiatt/Getty Images; p. 89 John Leyba/The Denver Post via Getty Images; p. 91 Dan Mullan/Getty Images; p. 93 Michael Dodge/Getty Images.

About the Author

Emily Mahoney is the author and editor of over a dozen nonfiction books for young readers on various topics. She has a master's degree in Literacy from the University at Buffalo and a bachelor's degree from Canisius College in Adolescent Education and English. She currently teaches reading to middle school students and loves watching her students learn how to become better readers and writers. She enjoys reading, Pilates, yoga, and spending time with family and friends. She lives with her husband in Buffalo, New York, where she was born and raised.